EΣ

Part one of the Exodus Trilogy

EXODUS

Andreas Christensen

EXODUS

Second edition

Copyright © Andreas Christensen 2013

ISBN: 978-1482320794

Cover design by Graphicz X Designs,

graphiczxdesigns.zenfolio.com

Editor: Shelley Holloway, hollowayhouse.me

This one is for Jonas and Siri

EXODUS

Prologue

Years ago, far too many to remember, the planet had been teeming with life. Its inhabitants had called it Lifebringer, and thousands of species had carved out their existence there. It was a finely tuned system, where every little being had its part to play. Lifebringer was part of a large family, a system of planets, moons, and asteroids dancing around their twin stars. Every rock had its place, and nothing had disturbed it for so long, it was taken for granted that this dance would go on eternally.

Nothing lasts forever though. The twin stars aged and slowly converged upon each other until one day they merged in a cataclysm that ended the dance, ruined entire worlds, and scattered the planets and their moons in every direction. Lifebringer, once the third planet from the larger of the twin stars, survived the cataclysm, but an enormous force pushed it out from its home and into the vast reaches of space. It was alone, and although it didn't know it, such planets would later become known as rogue planets, orphans in the eternity of space. Light dimmed and, over the years, disappeared completely. The surface got colder, and in time no life remained there. But the planet itself found no rest.

Space is vast and empty, and the stars few and far between, so the planet continued on, aimlessly and without purpose. Years became decades, decades became centuries, and centuries became millennia. Lifebringer had forgotten its past, its family not even a faint memory, doomed to an existence in the dark void between stars, with nowhere to call home.

Then one day, by pure chance, a star appeared. The rogue did not recognize the star, but its warm yellow glow called to it, and Lifebringer seemed on course toward it. Soon the planet could feel the force of the star pulling it in and was only too happy to let the star lead on; finally it had found a new home. And soon enough, it could feel, sometimes even see, its new family members; the small, frozen rocks far from their mother star; the gas giants, the ones with the magnificent rings; the moons dancing happily around their parents. So full of life, perfectly coordinated, such a wonderful family! Yes, this was where Lifebringer would settle, finally, after so long.

Then a small red planet appeared, and the rogue immediately realized its dreams of a new home had come to an end. There would be no peace, only destruction, a second cataclysm. For the red one had moved into its path, and none of them would survive such an impact. There was nothing more to do, no way to avoid the impact. An instant of regret, then nothing.

Chapter 1

November 2072 ~ North Africa

The fuel indicator was almost in the red, and Air Force pilot Tina Hammer worried that she would have to eject from her scramjet. She didn't relish the idea, although it would be better than taking her chances landing the plane somewhere in the desert. You could do that with the old jets and have a decent shot at getting through it alive, but with a scramjet, only a fool would try. The rocket had damaged much of her navigation equipment, along with the comms, of course, but she had a decent idea of where she was. Even without instruments, if she could just reach the coast within the next two minutes, she would be able to find the airfield by sight. She scanned the horizon from left to right. Nothing yet. Damn. The wound in her thigh didn't sting anymore, and she knew why. Blood loss. She knew that would kill her just as dead as a crash landing if she didn't land soon.

Then another bleep on her still-functional radar. Heat seeker. Shit. She still had some toys left, but releasing them would surely make other enemy patrols in the area aware of her position. She had obviously been picked up by at least one enemy with surface-to-air capacity, and she was all too aware that there were many other enemy factions down there who might be able to detect her presence if she were to take evasive action. Though her plane was crippled, the stealth features of the scramjet were still intact and could still have some value. Ah well, what choice did she have? Why worry about what could happen later, when you could get blown up now? She released the chaff, which should lure the heat seeker into the metal cloud, and spun the plane in a counterclockwise spiraling maneuver. Seconds felt like minutes. She'd done this more times than she cared to remember, and though she always acted cool and rational under pressure, she knew that once she got back, the shakes would come. She never told anyone of course. Her squadron was the best of the best, and if she confessed to such a thing, she could kiss any chance of flying scramjets again good-bye. And of course, as a black female pilot, even though both racial and gender discrimination had been illegal for ages— even in the military, and even though racial discrimination wasn't much of an issue anymore, she did feel she had to prove her worth as a pilot, over and over again. No, she always came out on top, and she would again. Whatever it takes, she thought, as the plane leveled.

The heat seeker exploded in the cloud of chaff behind her just as she caught a glimpse of the Mediterranean. She let out a breath of relief and felt the wound sting again. The plane was still stable, thank God, and as she turned left, she knew that she'd make it back once more. The airfield was less than a minute away, and although she was unable to call the tower, they would be expecting her. The landing strip would be clear, and the medics would be waiting. She gritted her teeth. As long as she didn't pass out now, she would be able to land the plane manually. This wasn't any ordinary job, but it was what she did for a living. And in a few days she would do it all over again.

November 2072 ~ Washington, DC

The phone rang just as Trevor Hayes had slumped into his favorite chair to watch the ballgame that would be coming on in just a few minutes.

"This is Hayes," he answered impatiently. As a Pegasus executive he was expected to be on call twenty-four hours a day, but at the moment, they weren't involved in activities that warranted that. Of course, it could be a journalist ...

"This is the White House. Please hold for the president." What is this? he thought. He'd spoken to the president twice, but only a few polite phrases at formal occasions. He didn't have much time to think, as a voice he was familiar with—mostly from TV—greeted him.

"Trevor, so nice to finally get to talk to you again."

"Mr. President."

"Oh don't be so formal, Trevor. I'll cut to the chase." He paused for a second, and Trevor had time to think that President Andrews would probably be restructuring his administration now that he'd just been reelected. "I want you on board. I need a new national security advisor, and I want someone who's not too political. I know you're a man I can trust, and you have the experience I'm looking for." Trevor was stunned.

"Mr. Pres … Ah, surely you have more qualified …" The president cut him off.

"What I don't need is another bureaucrat. You know politics, or well enough. Don't try to deny it. I've seen you coming up, you know." Andrews chuckled, and Trevor was lost for words. "So, my position is this. I need everything you know, and what you don't know you will learn. I have faith in you, young man. So be at the White House tomorrow at eight sharp. I'll let the staff know."

The line went dead and Trevor was still too stunned to think straight. Of course he'd take the job. No one refused the president of the United States. It was overwhelming, sure. But he'd been under fire enough times to know that when things get overwhelming, you need to take a step back and review the situation. Distance sometimes brings clarity, and, usually, things work out. As the ballgame began, Trevor realized he wouldn't be able to concentrate, so he turned it off.

Kenneth Taylor was sitting in an old leather chair on the ninth floor of William James Hall, where the historical exhibit of the Psychology Department was located. The department had a proud history, with names such as James, Munsterberg, Skinner, and Allport, and it still stood as one of the top research institutions in the country. When he first set foot in the building as an undergraduate, he had been a confident kid, on his way to fame and fortune. But over the years, he'd come to realize that the road to fame and fortune was littered with obstacles, and some might just send you on a different course than the one you'd set out on. He'd been a different man altogether back then, but some things never changed, like his respect for the classics in the field. He could think of no one he admired as much as the pioneer himself, William James. The stream of consciousness, the theories on choice and the will, the James-Lange theory of emotions—all important and groundbreaking. His theories were part of the foundation on which psychology had grown into its own, and it had happened right here, at Harvard. The building, although old enough to house the laboratory of B.F. Skinner, was much younger than the department itself, but nevertheless history permeated the walls here.

It was here that Kenneth used to come on occasion, all by himself, and just think. As a professor of the department, he was allowed access to the areas usually closed to both students and outsiders, and even most faculty members. He thought it was a shame, but at least he got to have a quiet moment here now and then. Some researchers would spend evenings in their offices, but here no one would bother him. On this particular night, he was reading an article on his tablet, obviously written by some ambitious journalist bent on getting the goodwill of his editors and the network owners. It was an article on the second reforms conducted by President Andrews's administration, and it was an utter disgrace to the once so self-respecting Fourth Estate. It was pure praise, and Kenneth grumbled beneath his thick, black beard. Andrews had led the charge and revised the Constitution until it was all but unrecognizable, and then this little bootlicker went out of his way to explain to the readers why it had been not just necessary, but desirable. Of course, within these walls, in the solitude of his own company, he could grumble all he wanted. But such carelessness anywhere else might quickly put an end to his career, or worse. This wasn't the America he once knew, but he'd seen it coming for years. And the sad thing was that most people felt good about it all. That somehow trampling the rights of ordinary people would protect them. The terrorists won after all, he thought to himself. They frightened us to the core after Seattle, and then we destroyed ourselves by removing choice.

November 2072 ~ Los Angeles, California

Maria Solis had never had a boyfriend. At the age of sixteen, a high school junior, this bothered her, but she didn't know what to do about it. Her friends always seemed to be dating, having boyfriends, and breaking up with them. There was always this sense of drama in their lives, and she felt that she was missing out on something, even though she couldn't tell exactly what it was. She wondered if there was something wrong with her.

"What's wrong with me?" she'd once asked Elle, who'd just giggled and strayed from the subject. Sometimes she thought her friend was shallow, but then again she had her moments.

"You're not a loner, Maria," Elle had told her when she'd brought up the subject again. "You're just difficult to get to know." Maria nodded, knowing that she tended to avoid the social settings that divided the students into groups and cliques.

"I just don't feel comfortable playing games."

A while ago, there were rumors in school saying she was a lesbian; but no, she did like boys, and thinking about girls that way didn't feel comfortable.

"You're beautiful, Maria. The boys don't know what they're missing!" That was Elle for you, making a joke out of everything. Maria shook her head.

"It's not that, it's just... I sometimes feel like time is running out," she said. "Class of '74, you know. Graduation's just a year and a half away. And so far, high school hasn't been all that I hoped for." She sighed. Once she graduated, she would go to college, of course. And with her parents being who they were, she expected she would be sent to a prestigious Ivy League university, where there would be no room for anything except her studies. She felt ambivalent thinking about that. On the one hand, she loved studying, and could immerse herself in the books on her tablet for hours and hours. She was a straight-A student, and though most of her studies came easily, she was also a hard worker. On the other hand, she knew there was more to life, and wondered if she would regret having spent so many evenings studying while her friends were out dating or just plain having fun.

"You have a good life, you know," Elle said. This time she didn't giggle or joke about it. Maria nodded, suddenly ashamed. She knew she had many opportunities that were denied others. She had loving parents, would receive a good education, and when she decided she was ready to take on business responsibilities, she was even the heir to one of the world's largest and most prosperous companies. Still, it all felt somewhat predictable, like her path had already been chosen for her. Not that her parents wouldn't let her make her own choices, of course. But still …

"I know, it's just that… I want to feel excited about something. I want to have some direction. I remember the stories grandpa used to tell me before he died. He would sit me on his lap and tell me about his dreams when he was young. He said he'd always dreamed of becoming an astronaut."

Elle seemed to be listening—and interested, so Maria continued her story. "He told me that when he first came to this country, men were preparing to go to Mars. The entire universe seemed open for exploration. It was an exciting time." Maria had always loved hearing about the old days; they had grand dreams back then, and she wanted to feel that same excitement and a dream to pursue.

"He said that when he saw John Scott set foot upon the red planet, he cried and believed anything was possible then." She could still remember the dreamy look in her grandpa's eyes. It made him look sort of sad.

The rest was history; the space dream ended when they tried to colonize Mars. Mr. Allred, her history teacher, had called the disaster a national trauma, from which they had never really recovered. He was right, and her grandpa's dream was dead long before he died himself. But she had never been able to forget the sparkle in his eyes. Elle wouldn't understand. No one would. These days nobody dreamed of space anymore. Remembering her grandpa, Maria sometimes wondered which was better: not seeing your dream come true, or not dreaming at all.

Chapter 2

December 2072 ~ Washington, DC

Running for an hour every morning had been part of his daily routine for years, and it was one of those things he always tried to find time for even with his busy schedule. It was getting chilly outside, even though DC in December could be a lot colder. He loved the freshness in the air that could only be found early, while most people were still sleeping soundly. Less than two weeks had passed since he'd been appointed national security advisor, and Trevor Hayes still felt a little overwhelmed by it all. He had almost completed his run when the cell phone rang. He looked at it, and saw it was President Andrews. What did the boss want this early? he thought.

"Mr. President," he said, breathing heavily.

"Trevor, something has come up," the president replied. "I need you in the Oval Office immediately. I'll have a car for you in two minutes, just stay where you are."

Of course, Hayes thought. *We're all being tracked and monitored these days. No reason for me to be exempt.* So he stretched for a couple of minutes before the black car with tinted windows drove up beside him. A secret service agent stepped out and opened the rear door for him. The agent said nothing as he entered, and they took him to the White House, driving a little too fast through the near empty streets.

Still wearing his running clothes, Trevor Hayes entered the Oval Office, where the president sat with an ashen face, staring at nothing. Beside him sat his chief of staff and the defense secretary, while the secretary of the interior, the secretary of the treasury, and the national science advisor stood. Another man Hayes hadn't seen before stood a little off to the back, fiddling with his papers. The president looked up at Trevor, and stood slowly.

"Come on in, Trevor. Why don't we just start, Charles?" The man at the back nodded, and flipped on a small projector device, and a second later an image of space appeared on the wall. He briefly introduced himself as Dr. Charles Quentin before he pointed at the image.

"This is an object that was discovered about a week ago, passing Jupiter at great speed. We weren't sure what it was until four days ago, when we identified it as a rogue planet." The defense secretary interrupted him and leaned forward.

"Dr. Quentin, if I may ask, what is a rogue planet?"

"A rogue planet is basically a planet without a star. The concept has always been controversial, although ESA confirmed their existence years ago. They are hard to find out there, but there may be as many as twice the number of stars. Now, rogue planets can be divided into two classes, although I'm not sure it's a very valuable distinction. First, we have those that were formed just like stars, kind of like brown dwarves. Then there are planets that were ejected from their star systems, due to some cataclysmic event, like a star going supernova or twin stars colliding." He clicked to another image. "This was taken yesterday. It's an image of Mars." Another click, and this time the image showed some sort of cloud, with a bigger dot near the middle of the cloud. "This image was taken just a few hours ago. This cloud is all that is left of Mars, and the object you can see as that dot right here …" He pointed at the dot in the middle. "This is the remains of the rogue planet." Silence filled the room as they took in the image of what had been Mars just yesterday. An entire planet gone. Hayes felt stunned.

"The rogue planet did that? There's nothing left of Mars, for Christ's sake." the president exclaimed. Dr. Quentin just nodded, and clicked again, and an enhanced image of the same scene appeared.

"The rogue planet crashed directly into Mars about twelve hours ago. Mars was completely destroyed by the impact, and the rogue planet lost most of its mass, except this large rock, about a hundred kilometers in diameter. Some of the debris will fall back onto the remains of the rogue, while some of it will remain as a cloud surrounding it for years. Some of it will escape the rogue's gravitational field and spread out."

"What if that had been Earth?" the secretary of the interior said quietly in a thin voice. Hayes instinctively knew the answer to that, and Dr. Quentin addressed the secretary's question.

"Even though Earth is larger than Mars, the result would have been the same. Total destruction. It's not just the size of the object, but also the velocity. The speed of that thing must have been enormous." He advanced to another image, but Hayes couldn't see that it was any different from the previous one. "This last image was taken just two hours ago. It tells us that the remains of the rogue have entered into a solar orbit, and it seems it's not far from the former orbit of Mars. We do expect it to differ some though, because when objects crash like this, the larger object will push more than the smaller one. And, like I said, there is the issue of velocity.

So its new orbit may turn out to be a bit closer to Earth than the one Mars followed. It's too early to tell, really."

"Why didn't we see this coming?" the president asked.

"Well, sir, these things are hard to detect. And its speed was like nothing I've ever seen before. Of course, it does make you think, doesn't it?" That last remark was one the scientist would regret, Hayes thought. He knew how all space-related activity had been severely handicapped by the aftermath of the Mars incident years earlier, and the subsequent disbanding of NASA and several other entities involved. In the U.S. there were barely any astronomers left, and those few worked on meager budgets with poor equipment and very little of the prestige the discipline once commanded. The U.S. got practically all their information from ESA these days. And most people paid no attention to space anyhow. People were simply not interested.

"How soon will we know what the object's orbit will look like?" the national science advisor asked.

"Well, that may take some time. In a few days we can have an estimate, but it may take a while before its orbit is stable. There is a chance that the new object may not be able to enter a stable orbit. In that case it will most likely be pulled in by the sun's gravity."

"It will hit the sun, is that what you are saying?" the secretary of defense asked, obviously disturbed by the possibility.

"Yes, but don't worry. The object wouldn't affect the sun, not even slightly. Compared to the sun, this is a speck of sand." Hayes thought about the object slowly being swallowed up by the sun, and suddenly got an unpleasant idea. He had to ask.

"Is there any chance that, if the object doesn't enter a stable orbit, it may hit Earth?" The others obviously hadn't thought of the possibility, and quite a few heads turned toward him. The scientist merely chuckled and shook his head.

"Highly unlikely, sir. I'd say the chances of that thing coming anywhere near us are one in a million. Less, probably. I wouldn't worry about it." Hayes nodded slowly. He was probably right. But what had the chances been that it would hit Mars?

December 2072 ~ Los Angeles, California

Maria and Elle were sitting in the high school cafeteria. Maria was picking absently at her food, while Elle was eyeing the boys at a table nearby. A history assignment Maria had been working on the night before had made her think of her grandfather, and she had thought about him even as she lay in bed, far too late for a Tuesday, while sleep evaded her. The memory still lingered in the back of her mind.

"Did you complete the essay on the first Mars Expedition, Elle?" she asked her friend sitting next to her. They had been given the task of writing an essay on the first manned expedition to Mars, and to her surprise, she had found reading up on it to be exciting. She'd never been much into space in general, and she wasn't alone. Society had no interest in space exploration anymore. But, reading about it reminded her of her grandfather's stories and his dreams of space exploration. The failed Mars colony had shown that man belonged on Earth; at least that's what everybody said. But the story of humans in space had its place in the history books, and as Mr. Allred always said: we study history to learn from our mistakes. She did like history, particularly modern history, so maybe it was the historical angle—and the memory of her grandfather—that attracted her to the story of how John Scott was the first human ever to set foot on Mars, back in 2038.

"Yuck, I tried, but it's just so boring! I don't understand why we have to learn all that Mars stuff. We all know how that ended up, so let's leave it at that." Obviously satisfied with her own statement, Elle nodded to herself and looked over at the table where Charlie and Bill, both on the football team, were sitting. "You know, Maria, it's just a month and a half to go. I sure hope Bill gets off his butt and asks me soon. He should, you know; I have options." She was talking about the New Year's dance again. Elle was a popular girl, and had already been asked by three guys, but she still waited for Bill, the quarterback, to ask her. "What about you? Has anybody asked you yet?" Maria just shook her head. "Maria, I swear, I don't understand boys. I don't think any of the boys here really know you. Or maybe they think they won't be able to talk to you, or something." Maria felt her cheeks flushing; she wished Elle didn't have to be so loud.

"Elle … I don't know … Let's just finish our lunch and go. I need to deliver a note from my parents to the dean's office. I'm supposed to go with them to New York next Friday. Dad's going to his quarterly meeting with his business associates, but Mom's not attending. I guess that means she and I will go Christmas shopping." She smiled, thinking that her mother would definitely take advantage of the opportunity to get away from her normally hectic pace at the office. Isabella Solis always had a role in the major business decisions for the company, even though Maria's father, Ramon, was the CEO. So Ramon going to a big quarterly meeting with other corporate leaders without her was something out of the ordinary.

Ramon and Isabella were descendants of poor immigrants from Mexico. Their parents had all come illegally to the United States and were among the many who, in the great amnesty of 2030, became legal permanent residents, but without the citizenship. It was this status that had kept Ramon's father from being able to fulfill his dream of becoming an astronaut.

Since Ramon and Isabella had been born in America, they were citizens of the United States, and worked hard to make their way in the business world. They had started a small online business from home, which turned out to be a huge success, and, within just a few years, it had grown into a large corporation. Now Cheevo was one of the largest corporations in America, with branches on all continents.

Once, when Maria was about five, she had asked what their company made. Ramon had laughed fondly, and explained to her that they didn't actually make anything. Cheevo was involved in a lot of different industries; they managed and leased copyrights for intellectual property, they financed other startup companies, and they now had several scientific research centers around the world. At the time, Maria didn't understand any of it, of course, but she knew she had to learn some day. One day she would inherit the company. Her parents, though loving and gentle people, had great expectations of her and demanded that she work hard at school, so that when the day came, she'd be ready to take the reins.

"I still think you should try to get Charlie to take you to the New Year's dance!" Elle said, loudly enough for the whole cafeteria to hear, or so it felt. Maria nudged her hard with her elbow as they walked out the doors, both girls giggling.

December 2072 ~ Washington, DC

It had been a week since the rogue planet had annihilated Mars, and the world had been taken by surprise. During that week, it had been the biggest story on every news site. Everybody talked about it, and although people were shocked that something like this could actually happen, they were also relieved that it had been Mars, and not Earth, that had been hit. One of the issues that had made headlines was the fact that there had been virtually no warning. In the late twentieth and early twenty-first centuries, the possibility of a meteor strike or an asteroid hitting Earth had been given a lot of attention, so although interest had been virtually zero for years now, the idea that something might fall out of the sky to wreak havoc on Earth was nothing new. The thing that made this such a frightening, sensational story worldwide, besides the scale of it all, was its late discovery. In the past, people had expected to have at least weeks, if not months of warning before an asteroid or meteor impact. The possibility that an object like the rogue planet could suddenly just appear out of nowhere and, within a week, destroy an entire planet had caused a lot of debate.

In the aftermath of the Mars incident back in the sixties, the American components of the Spaceguard Survey were largely disbanded, and although some foreign institutions still conducted their own surveys, the number of Near Earth Objects discovered had decreased drastically. Although the media exercised a great deal of self-censorship these days, this latest development was one they couldn't shy away from, and even government representatives were calling for a renewed effort to protect the world from possible impacts, such as this one. Although no one could imagine how to protect Earth from something as massive as a rogue planet, most agreed that some sort of renewed Spaceguard Survey should be considered.

The remaining slab of rock from the rogue planet was treated as a new minor planet. There were discussions about whether it would stay in orbit or be pulled into the sun, and the one-in-a-million chance of an impact with Earth held very little interest, except as a curiosity. A small minority worried, but they were mostly loons and doomsday preachers; good for laughs, but nobody took them seriously. Mars had saved us all, it was said. And although the red planet on which man had once walked would be missed by some, most paid more attention to the rock that now remained. As soon as the story of the destruction of Mars spread, the rock had been given a name. But the scientists naming such an object obviously didn't have a sense of communication, so *The Washington Post* held a twenty-four-hour naming contest. The name that got the most votes was less fanciful than several others, but it was easily recognizable and conveyed an important part of its recent history. It was quickly adopted by others, and when even the president mentioned it by its new name, the name stuck. The object's name was Devastator.

Since the story broke, there had been daily briefings in the Oval Office on the situation. As Trevor Hayes sat down for the daily briefing, he noticed that Dr. Quentin was absent. Another scientist, a younger Asian woman, had replaced him, and she had a look on her face that was difficult to interpret. The president himself was the last to enter, and as soon as he had greeted them all and sat down, the new scientist introduced herself as Dr. Linda Xiu.

"As you know, we have been working round the clock trying to learn everything we can about Devastator. I'm not going to repeat the information already given to you by Dr. Quentin, as most of it is correct." She paused for a second, and when the president urged her on, she still took her time about it. Then she dropped the bomb.

"Devastator may hit us, after all." She ignored the reactions and continued.

"Like I said, Dr. Quentin was right about a lot of things. But to be absolutely clear, the chances of a direct impact by Devastator are not one in a million at all. It now seems that Devastator has settled into an orbit that will take it steadily closer to the sun, meaning also that it will come closer to Earth. We were calculating how the orbits of Earth and Devastator compared, when we found that at one of the points where the orbits cross each other, there will be an impact. There is a slight chance it will only be an extremely close encounter, meaning that it will enter Earth's atmosphere, but escape Earth's gravitational pull due to its speed. However, the likelihood of such an outcome is shrinking by the hour, as we gather more and more data.

"It's important that you get some idea of the scale we're talking about. The diameter of the object that most likely wiped out the dinosaurs was, according to the latest theories, somewhere in the vicinity of ten kilometers in diameter. That doesn't seem like a lot, considering the size of Earth, but that impact caused a brief heat wave that killed a lot of animals and plant life. It probably caused huge tsunamis and earthquakes worse than you can imagine as well, and there is evidence of increased volcanism that corresponds with the time of impact. But the real extinction event wasn't the impact itself, but the long-term effects, when dust particles from the impact clouded the sky for years, decades maybe, and temperatures dropped rapidly. Winter for years, starvation … All that from an object of about ten kilometers in diameter." She paused for a second to let it sink in.

"Devastator is ten times that size." The room was silent now. They had just been told that something ten times the size of what killed the dinosaurs would most likely hit Earth some time during the next few years. Hayes was the first to speak.

"You said 'one of the points where the orbits cross.' What did you mean?" Dr. Xiu flicked on the projector and started an animation that showed the orbits of both Earth and Devastator, with a timer that showed the month and year of each position. They could see with their own eyes how Devastator's orbit slowly spiraled inward, and after eight years, the orbits crossed each other, close but not an impact yet. This continued for another four years before the animation stopped, and the word "impact" labeled the point where the two converged. Dr Xiu explained it for them.

"As you can see, in about eight years, the orbits will cross, and it will be quite close, so we might experience some effects even then, such as smaller objects, debris from the impact between the rogue and Mars, bombarding Earth, there may be strange weather phenomena, and so forth. We need to work a little more on that to give more accurate estimates.

Four years later, sometime near the end of 2084, we expect a direct impact to take place." The president, quite affected by the news, rose and shook Dr. Xiu's hand.

"Thank you, ma'am. Ah, we will talk more later, I think. Now, if you will excuse me, I need to speak to my advisors in private." She nodded, picked up her notes, and left the room. As she closed the door behind her, President Andrews turned toward the others still sitting in their chairs. He looked pale and obviously shocked, just as everyone else, and seemed desperate to find his bearing again. Unsuccessfully, Hayes thought.

"I want you all to keep this quiet. I mean that, not one word! That message will go out to the scientists too. If … if this information spreads, there will be panic and riots. Panic and riots, you understand, right? The perfect conditions for terrorists and other destructive elements. We must keep this a secret for as long as possible. That will give us some time to come up with a plan for how to deal with all this." He sat, or rather slumped, down again, and Hayes noticed his knuckles, white as he held on to the table as if he would fall off his chair if he didn't hold tightly enough.

"We need to set up a meeting as soon as possible, I think." The president didn't look much like the authority figure he was known to be, and his voice had turned shaky and a note higher than usual. He nodded to himself, biting his lip.

"I think … George Havelar … I'll have someone call Havelar later today. He needs to attend the meeting. And the other loyal business leaders, too. Havelar will find a way, I know he will."

Chapter 3

December 2072 ~ New York City, New York

Ramon Solis had just turned forty this past week, and it had felt weird. It was as if he were standing outside his own body, looking at himself from a short distance, and not recognizing who he'd become. Somehow, and this had been coming for some time now, he felt estranged from himself. He knew he was having some kind of midlife crisis, but hoped he wouldn't do something ridiculous, like buy a motorcycle or get a mistress, as so many others tended to do when they suddenly looked at themselves in the mirror and saw their own mortality staring back at them. His wife, two years younger, coped so well with his current weirdness; he wondered how she did it.

It was the quarterly meeting of the heads of some of the largest and most successful businesses in the country, and they were, as usual, gathered at the Havelar Industries headquarters in New York. His wife and daughter had followed him, to take the opportunity to enjoy some of the things that only New York could offer. Right now they were Christmas shopping, and later they would go to a Broadway show that he couldn't remember the name of. As the other business leaders came in and sat down at the large conference table, Ramon found himself feeling a bit uneasy not having Isabella with him. They usually made all major decisions together, but she had wanted to spend some time with Maria this time. They needed to talk about college, she'd said.

Havelar Industries was one of several large corporations that had emerged within the last couple of decades to become the engine driving the new American economy, which had been struggling for years with competition from Asian and South American economies, especially after the fall of the Chinese communist party. Cheevo was another, and like Havelar Industries, Cheevo and several other corporations had gradually, over the last few years, grown into a network that also included the former Holloway administration, as well as Andrews's current administration. Since most of the old antitrust laws had been largely abandoned, and private-public cooperative projects were now the model for the new American economy, the network wasn't as much of a legal issue as it would have been in the twentieth or early twenty-first century. But still it was something that wasn't spoken about outside the inner circle of the Consortium, which had become the unofficial name of the network.

The Consortium's ties to government didn't just mean large government contracts; it also meant a steady flow of information, sometimes long before the information reached the public, or even outer parts of the government apparatus. This was just another regularly scheduled quarterly meeting, and normally a representative from the government would attend, but Ramon was taken by surprise when the president entered the room. Right next to the president, a solemn George Havelar entered the room, followed by the secretary of the interior, the defense secretary, the national security advisor, the president's science advisor, and at last a man he recognized as the old JPL Director Daniel Shaw. The president only attended the meetings himself when the topics were particularly important, and this unprecedented entourage indicated that this meeting would be something out of the ordinary. What in the world would make the president bring in the former JPL director? The Jet Propulsion Laboratory was but a shadow of its former greatness, an anachronism gathering dust out in Pasadena.

They all greeted each other with polite and sometimes warm smiles and handshakes, although Havelar, President Andrews, and his people smiled less than usual, and they all had that somber expression on their faces more commonly seen at funerals than business meetings in the new economy. Again, Ramon got a feeling that this was anything but a business meeting. And then another thing happened that was contrary to etiquette. When the president occasionally attended meetings of the Consortium, it was customary that he opened the meeting, before Havelar, as the elected chairman, took over. This time, however, it was Havelar who stood up and took charge.

"This is the most important meeting you will ever attend." It was a short and blunt statement that immediately got the attention of every person in the room. Havelar let it hang in the air for a few seconds before he continued.

"What you are about to be told is the worst news you could possibly imagine, probably worse. I'm sorry about that. After you are presented with all the information that currently exists, we will have a discussion, a very important discussion. The results of that discussion will set the course for every corporation represented in this room, for the government, and for all our lives for years to come. It will be like a pact, and it will bind us all together, more than ever. I know I can trust you all to keep quiet about what is said in this room today. And when I say quiet, I mean it. Not a word to your wives, husbands, kids, your closest friends, anyone. Get it?" They all nodded, slowly. None hesitated about the secrecy; they just wondered what could cause Havelar to be so … Ramon was unable to find the right way to put it. He just got a very bad feeling about it all, and once again wished Isabella had been here with him.

"So, having said that, I'll let the president's science advisor tell you what's going on." He turned toward the short, balding man to the president's left, whose ashen face matched that of his superior. "I can't say I envy you the task, Harry, but however that may be, you're the messenger ..."

The science advisor rose slowly from his chair, took out a small projector, and set it up facing the white wall at the front of the room, so that everyone could see. The first image to appear was one of a starry sky, with one tiny white dot having a red ring drawn around it.

"Ah ... You've all seen this in the news for the last few weeks. This is Devastator's position at the moment ... What you see here isn't 100 percent correct, as the image has been both enhanced and magnified. Devastator reflects very little light, and it's hard to see if you don't know where it is. For the time being." He took a sip of water before he continued.

"As I said, you've probably seen a lot of these images on the news." A new image appeared on the wall, this time of Devastator and the cloud of debris surrounding it.

"A week ago, we believed that Devastator would either find an orbit close to that of Mars, or be sucked in by the sun's gravitational pull, and that would be the end of it. Now we know better. Devastator is on a spiraling course inward toward the sun. The bad news is that our orbit and that of Devastator will converge in a few years." He paused for a second. When he saw that not everyone had realized what he'd just said, he rephrased.

"It's coming our way, folks."

Twenty minutes later, the presentation ended with the image of Devastator still projected on the wall, and Ramon couldn't take his eyes away from that image of impending doom. The room had gone completely silent. Not even Havelar spoke. Finally, one of the other business leaders spoke, in a shaky voice.

"Is there anything we can do? What about our nuclear rockets, if we launched them all at once, maybe we could divert it? Or, I once saw a documentary about a scheme to divert comets with lasers ..." He was abruptly interrupted by Havelar.

"Forget about missiles and fucking laser defenses. It wouldn't even kiss the surface of this thing, and to divert it, we'd have had to discover it years before now. It simply can't be done. So forget about all those fancy schemes. It seems a few other nations have seen what's coming too, and they're planning all kinds of futile countermeasures. In fact, the Chinese and the Russians are fantasizing about the very comet-diverting notion you just mentioned. I guess they've seen the same TV shows ... Ah, hell, as long as they're not pointing those nukes at us ... And while we're at it, forget about holing up underground too; it simply will not make a difference either way. We're talking earthquakes, tsunamis, nuclear winter or whatever you'd like to call it. Shit, you name it, it's coming." As the message sank in, Havelar got up from his chair and walked around the table to stop right next to the JPL director. Ramon, having known Havelar for years now, knew that meant something. George Havelar never did anything unintentionally.

"Let's be clear about this, folks," he continued. "There is no defense we could possibly put up that would stand a chance at stopping this fucker. All we can hope for here, what our survival as a species depends upon, is that the time we have and the combined resources of the Consortium and the government are enough that a small number, probably a very small number, can slip away. To where, and how, has yet to be decided. But as I just told you, what we should be thinking about here is the survival of our species.

Most of us will die. If we can save a hundred or a thousand doesn't matter. Of humanity, the billions left on earth will die. Their only motivation will be to save the handfuls that will go."

A purpose then, Ramon thought. That's what this meeting is about. Not just painting the face of doom up on the wall. Now, that's the genius of George Havelar. While the president and his advisors were still recovering from shock, too stunned to do anything at all, let alone devise any sort of productive action, Havelar already had a plan in his mind. It was probably still just a loose framework, but the contours were there, and although bordering on impossible, Havelar never set out to do anything he couldn't achieve. He undoubtedly already had dozens of people working on mission design, feasibility analyses, and so forth. Ramon smiled to himself, as he couldn't help admire the absolute genius of the man who just a few years ago was featured on the front of *Time* magazine as Man of the Year. He turned from his inner musings to listen to Havelar again.

"Earth will be dead, one way or the other, in less than twelve years. So, basically, what we have to do is to build an ark. A group of carefully selected people in a large tin can, with the world's most powerful nuke or some kind of sci-fi rocket strapped to their asses, will be catapulted into space to find somewhere to settle down, to build a civilization from scratch somewhere on some distant rock." He paused as he took a deep breath.

The security advisor, a clean-cut man in his forties, of military bearing and demeanor, opened his mouth for the first time. When he did, his voice was steady; he seemed determined to assess each angle, and Ramon immediately took a liking to this man. Actually, the man surprised him, because most of the government types had seemed more or less paralyzed.

"That is, if we can get there before the ship breaks down." He looked around at every one of them, and made sure he had their full attention, before he continued.

"You know, there are myriad details, and a small failure in any one of them would mean certain death. Unless we can think of it beforehand and make sure it doesn't happen."

The science advisor cut in, still sweaty from his presentation, but with a determined look upon his face. He pushed back his glasses that constantly threatened to dive off the tip of his nose, yet that very move made him seem a lot more comfortable now.

"We'd need multiple redundancies in most areas just to stand a decent chance of surviving even the smallest unforeseen event." He scribbled a few hasty notes on his tablet and continued hastily.

"And the time frame limits our options dramatically. Sure, we might be close to a breakthrough in FTL travel, biotech might in just a few years expand a human life span to be several times what we consider natural age today, and the latest surgical techniques suggest ways of halting metabolism in such ways that people could literally be frozen for centuries before being revived whenever the ship arrives. But as you all know, we don't have the luxury of time.

"We need to determine how long we can reasonably expect to have to develop our solution, because at some point we'll see a lot of obstacles appearing. One of those obstacles will be the political situation, should all this come out. Who knows whether a ship with just a select few people on board would even be able to launch once people realize they won't be among the few who will go? There is no telling what the situation will be when people get desperate. Most of you will probably think we should use what we've got, and get off the planet A.S.A.P., just to make sure. That would be a grave mistake." The security advisor nodded, as did a few others, while most stared quizzically at him.

"But what if we wait too long?" one of the Consortium members asked. Ramon could see the point. What if some event made launch impossible, what would be the cost of that compared to having to solve a few problems en route? The science advisor just shook his head though.

"No, no, no. Leaving too soon is the worst thing we could do. On the contrary, we need to wait for as long as possible. Every day we have before departure will pay off in scientific knowledge, technological development, training, planning, preparing, etcetera. In space, resources are limited, and improvements will be much more difficult. Here, we still have abundant resources, much of the world's scientific and technological community at our disposal, and the luxury of making mistakes. We can take risks that would be impossible in space, and instead of a few hundred brains we have millions." Havelar interceded, obviously playing the devil's advocate.

"On the other hand, if we're not ready in time, we lose everything …."

The science advisor nodded at Havelar's remark and concluded, "So there is a need for balance, we need a timeframe that gives us the advantages of Earth-based R&D and production capacity, and at the same time allows those lucky few to get away before it all breaks down. Whatever we do, we cannot allow any one single issue to bog us down. Above all, we need forward movement. What we know is this: Impact will most likely happen approximately twelve years from now. Some of the effects of the close encounters prior to impact will hit us within eight years." Not very long, Ramon thought, to figure out how to send a viable population to another planet, build the necessary vehicle for transport, launch the ship, and wave good-bye.

"Somewhere in between years eight and twelve, we will encounter our point of no return, the day when we can no longer launch, and all our efforts will be in vain. If that happens, all we can do is pray." As the science advisor fell silent, Havelar again took charge.

"All right, so Devastator will hit us in a little more than a decade. Whether anyone survives the impact is a toss of the dice; the scientists cannot yet say for certain. But however that plays out, the destruction will be … well, impossible to describe … Mankind will most likely not survive the long-term effects, so it is up to us, here in this room, to make a plan that may save a tiny fraction of our species." This time, everyone nodded, some eagerly, and some still recovering from the bad news. Ramon again noticed that the president himself had been mostly passive, as if his mind was elsewhere. Now, President Andrews rose from his chair, and to everyone's surprise held up a piece of paper, as if he had already written a script that he intended to follow. Ramon was disturbed by the sight. Hadn't he listened to the others at all? The president began, and it immediately became apparent that he had a lot of concerns that had little to do with the task at hand.

"When NASA so horrendously failed at sustaining the Mars colony, it was merely the culmination of various missteps that had been going on for decades. Even the successful first manned flight to Mars couldn't change the fact that NASA had become a symbol of the past, of the weaknesses and lack of vision that so entrenched this country for years, and that the terrorists took advantage of. All those things happened before the reforms that ended bureaucratic practices. And those reforms made it possible for decisive men to take charge and save this great democracy from its enemies, foreign and domestic." This was the official version of history these days, and something Ramon had heard before. He'd never quite become comfortable with those views, even if his own success had been built upon that of the reformed American government. And whatever he felt, he still couldn't see the relevance to the momentous efforts ahead. NASA was long dead, and to gather the expertise necessary for this, they would have to look elsewhere.

"The truth about Devastator is only known to a few people in this country, and for the time being, let's keep it that way. However, there are others who are already moving on this. As mentioned already, the Chinese and Russians are cooperating on a scheme to divert the course of the planet. And to no avail. They will fail miserably, have no doubt about it, and when they realize that, they will see that they have spent all their resources and gained nothing. The other great powers are somewhat of a mystery to us; we know that things are stirring in India, and they have extracted most of their best scientists that were working abroad, in the U.S., Europe, and South Africa. Clearly they intend to mount some kind of effort, we just don't know what. With their security policies, the Indian flow of information is close to zero. As for Brazil, we think they might do something similar to us, but they are being unusually tight lipped about it. The only ones we currently have an open channel to are the Europeans. ESA already have a team working on planetary habitability, trying to find a viable target planet, and we expect that they will soon be a full partner in our venture." The science advisor nodded, as did several others. They all knew that when NASA was disbanded and the study of space generally fell into disgrace, astronomy was one field of research that had lost influence and support in the United States. ESA had gone the other way, increasing their funding of astronomy programs, and were years ahead. Without their cooperation, any American mission would for all practical purposes be blind.

"The one thing I am skeptical about when it comes to the Europeans is the fact that they have very differing views on what to do with dissidents. There are elements in ESA that have been vocal enemies of our reforms, as if they had any right to concern themselves with our business. Clearly, they will have to be excluded from any joint projects. We don't want their destructive views to spread." The president let the sentence hang in the air, while silently challenging anyone to disagree. It had been a long time since anyone had spoken up about the kind of institutionalized paranoia the president seemed to display, so no one said anything. President Andrews, satisfied with the silence, continued.

"All right, so we need to maintain a level of security here. We will not share everything with the Europeans, but to obtain their cooperation, we need to reserve some seats on the spaceship for them. And we will make sure that their candidates go through the same selection process as our people, so that dissidents and leftists are properly weeded out.

There have to be some of their candidates we can approve of; they're not all bad, thank God. As for our American candidates, we'll perform thorough background checks to make sure we only send loyal people of like mind to build a new world. That same standard also has to apply to everyone working on the project, and especially the ones in charge of selecting the right candidates." Ramon noticed the national security advisor raised an eyebrow, before his face quickly became as blank and unreadable as before. The president walked over to where Daniel Shaw, the former director of JPL, was sitting and put his hands on Shaw's shoulders.

"Some of you may already have recognized Daniel Shaw, former director of JPL of Pasadena. JPL will play an important role, as it has done in several previous space endeavors of this country. When Congress investigated the Mars incident, JPL was shown to have foreseen ,many of the weaknesses that caused the mission to become such a tragedy. It was one of the few institutions involved that was not prosecuted or disbanded in the aftermath." He paused, and then smiled.

"When all that happened, Daniel was just a rocket engineer, of course, but he later came to be director, and his legacy is that of several successful military applications of the technology developed out in Pasadena. He's also a friend of mine, and one of the people I would trust with something as important as this. He will be in charge of the project and report back to me. The Consortium will be an advisory board that will be consulted on all major decisions. There will be plenty of work, and I expect each of you to already have some idea as to how your companies can contribute. If you have anything urgent, take it up with George." He nodded at Havelar, who nodded in acknowledgement. One of the business leaders, Dana Fuller of the high-tech Quantum Industries, raised her hand slowly, then spoke.

"We need to have a name. I guess we could just call it the project …" Havelar shook his head.

"Of course we need a name. A name that says something of the magnitude of the challenges we're talking about here, of the importance. To help us stay inspired."

"Exodus," Ramon said quietly, then as the room fell silent, he looked up to see everyone looking at him.

"That's what this is," he said, and several nodded, others murmured agreement. The president smiled; he was known to be a religious man.

"Exodus it is."

There was just a week left until Christmas, and Ramon knew it would be very different this year. Even though they had all pledged not to reveal anything to their families, spouses included, Isabella Solis, as much CEO as her husband but for the title, was the sole exception. But both knew their daughter had to be spared the burden of this knowledge. As a teenager, she had enough on her mind. Still, Ramon wondered what it would be like celebrating Christmas while knowing the world would soon come to an end.

Two days had passed since their last meeting. They were sitting around the same table, almost all the business leaders and the same representatives from the administration, except the president, who had to maintain an appearance to the public as if it was all business as usual. In addition, there were several scientists. Director Shaw had brought several from JPL, some former NASA people, and even a couple of astronomers from ESA who looked mighty jet-lagged. Ramon had brought his wife, Isabella, much to the dismay of Havelar, who agreed with the president that as few as possible should know, including family. Ramon had pushed it through though. Even Havelar had to give in to the fact that, although Ramon Solis was CEO of Cheevo, Isabella had always been a part of the Consortium meetings, speaking on Cheevo's behalf with as much weight as Ramon.

The meeting had begun half an hour ago, with a recap of previous events and the decision to establish Project Exodus. They all knew they were talking about sending people off Earth to make sure humanity could survive. But the details were blurry, as most of them had no idea where such an expedition could go, and few knew much about space at all. So the goal for the meeting was to come up with options for the scientists to continue working on.

As the walkthrough of the estimates for how Devastator would behave in the coming years drew to a close, Havelar again took charge, and repeated the question they were all pondering.

"So where do we go?" He looked at each and every one of them, and let the question linger for a moment before he continued.

"A viable Mars settlement was always the goal, and for all practical purposes the final destination for most of our space endeavors, at least before we disbanded NASA. After that … well, it was irrelevant. But now that Mars is gone, what options do we have?" One of the former NASA people,

Dr. Jacob Grant, a gray-haired man who now worked in the civilian satellite business, spoke first.

"Let's look at it this way. First, we need to explore the possibilities within the solar system. I mean, that's obvious. With current technology, anything else is a pipe dream. Second, further out, the stars. Of course, we're not able to do that today or tomorrow, but let's consider it anyhow. We're sort of brainstorming here, folks, we should look at every option, realistic or not. And besides, they didn't have the technology to send people to the moon in 1961 either. But they did it." One of the business leaders, looking rather puzzled, interrupted him.

"I don't know what you're thinking here, but I just don't get it. The solar system? Where? With Mars out of the equation now, I can't see where that would be." Grant smiled and nodded slowly.

"Actually, you have a point. It may not be possible to live anywhere else in the solar system. What I said was that we need to explore the possibilities, then take care of the obstacles, or rule out the reckless and the impossible." He sipped his water while the business leader quieted down.

"So, the solar system." Grant continued. "First off, we will need some way of harvesting resources, since supplies from Earth will not be an option. That makes Earth orbit a bad choice. The moon could be a possibility. It has encrusted oxygen, and minerals, all of which could be mined. The problem is that the moon has no atmosphere and very little water. Those are critical factors when it comes to long-term survival." Ramon looked over at Havelar, who seemed disinterested and a little annoyed at this point. Grant though, was clearly unaffected, and from the looks of the other scientists, his opinions seemed to carry a lot of weight.

"We could also imagine something like a space station, in orbit somewhere further out, or some kind of free-flying settlement in space." Eric Sloan, one of the engineers from JPL, shook his head while waving a finger back and forth, almost admonishing. A crinkle in the corners of his eyes, though, let anyone who bothered to look see that he was simply following Grant's line of thought.

"Let's not go down that road, Dr. Grant," said Sloan. "We could barely maintain the orbital stations, and we still had the luxury of ground supplies … We are simply not capable of building lasting, closed life-support systems. There will always be losses, and faults, and unforeseen contingencies. Eventually it will break down. What we need to aim for is something that will last long enough to get us somewhere." At that point Isabella surprised her husband by speaking.

"So, we need supplies, resources. That means planets, right?" That was Isabella Solis; quick to draw the conclusions, and not wasting time on further discussion when the outcome seemed obvious. The president's science advisor cut her off though.

"Let's not get ahead of ourselves, people. We have other options, so please let Dr. Grant continue." Grant smiled at Isabella before he continued.

"Oh, I think both Dr. Sloan and Mrs. Solis make good points. So no space habitats; we need to be able to replenish our resources at some point. The planets are an option, so are some of the moons orbiting Saturn or Jupiter. NASA found evidence of organic compounds on Titan ..." He halted, as a red-faced Havelar stood up and motioned for them all to stop talking.

"Goddammit, you guys. What the hell are you talking about? You all seem to forget one simple fact; we're human. We need open spaces, land to build upon, to multiply, to expand. Remember, this is about a new beginning, not finding some dark hole to hide out in. We should be looking at ways to create a possibility for life, not just some meaningless existence." Grant nodded, then several others followed suit. Ramon thought Grant looked like he'd planned this all from the start, and now he got to conclude his own line of reasoning, with all the downsides to the alternatives covered.

"I think it's safe to say now that we need to find a planet or a large moon which is Earth-like. I'm talking about size, gravity, temperature, water, oxygen, and atmosphere. With an atmosphere we don't have to wear pressure suits, although it doesn't have to be breathable. So let's be clear here. There is nothing remotely like that in our solar system, except Earth. So we're not talking about the solar system anymore. We're talking about sending a spaceship to some star system light years away. We're talking about a new Earth and a new beginning for mankind." The point seemed to sink in with everyone in the room now. Man had never travelled to the stars before, and now, as the survival of mankind itself was under threat, they would, in just a few years, send a starship on a one-way journey into deep space to find a new home for the survivors. The dimensions were staggering, and Ramon thought it all seemed surreal. Sloan from JPL again shook his head as he raised his concerns.

"I think everyone should be aware of the difficulties we're looking at here. There are so many questions that need answering. Where do we find this planet? How can we be sure it has all the properties we need? And what about space flight? We haven't even touched upon that. We're not talking chemical rockets here; we have to come up with entirely new methods of propulsion, and fast! How fast? Is it at all possible to come up with a way to travel to the stars? The engineering issues here are huge!" Havelar nodded at Sloan, a wide grin spreading across his face while his eyes got that look they often did when confronted with an obstacle no one quite knew how to handle.

"It's all frontier work from here, folks." He looked around, then at his watch, and smiled.

"I think we all need a break. This is a lot to take in, and I'd like us to address the issues one by one, or we'll get nowhere." Ramon and Isabella looked at each other. Isabella voiced a name with her lips, and Ramon found he'd been thinking about it, at least subconsciously, since he first heard what would happen on Earth in just a few years. Maria.

Chapter 4

Ramon had the feeling that he didn't belong; that he had no right to attend this meeting with so many highly qualified people. He didn't have any qualifications whatsoever for all this, although that went for some of the others too. There were about fifteen people in the room back at the Havelar Industries headquarters, and apart from George Havelar and Ramon Solis, who represented the Consortium, Daniel Shaw, director of Project Exodus, and the science advisor, all the others were scientists and engineers. He recognized Dr. Grant and Dr. Sloan, but all the others were unknown to him. Their objective for today was to come up with the number of people that could be carried on a starship to create a new beginning for mankind. It was important that they hit the right balance between so many different factors; it had to be within the limits of engineering, and at the same time it had to be as big as possible, in order to make sure the colony would be able to sustain itself, once they reached the new world.

"So, where do we begin?" one of the engineers asked. Ramon had no idea. How many people were needed to create a viable population? One of the scientists obviously seemed to know a little about that, as she took charge of the discussion immediately.

"Let's start by examining what kind of gene pool we need. That will give us a minimum number of people that would be able to breed." She continued to explain how they needed a population of at least a hundred people, a number supported by several studies on genetic diversity.

"Of course, such a minimum presupposes that we are able to have maximum genetic diversity, which means no relatives, and a pure genetic selection not hampered with other concerns, like skills." She paused for a second, as several of the attendees nodded knowingly.

"And if you think that's unrealistic, there's more. For a hundred people to be the nucleus of a healthy, genetically diverse breed of humans, there have to be no accidents. No illnesses, no early deaths. If cryo sleep were to have some kind of harmful side effects, or one of the shuttles crashed, or if we had a bad outbreak of influenza, that could seriously endanger the entire population. So in my view, a hundred people is the bare minimum, and it's still too risky. I would go for double of that, at least." As she leaned back, having said what she intended to say, Dr. Grant leaned forward.

"All right, so we have a minimum. Below that there ain't much point, right? Of course, some of my colleagues might point out that we've never built anything larger than the thirty-man shuttle, and that anything big enough to carry 100-plus would need to be developed gradually and over years. Forget it, won't happen. We're breaking new ground here. In my view, what we need to do is think compartments. We build compartments, parts of the starship, which by themselves cannot exceed the maximum payload of a certain number of shuttle launches. We make them as easy as possible to assemble, so that it could be done blindfolded if need be. All right, that's an exaggeration, but you know what I mean. We spend whatever needs spending in order to be finished on time, right?" He eyed Ramon and Havelar briefly, before he continued. Of course. He and Havelar were there to make sure the others understood that, whatever the cost, it would not be an issue. Being used to operating on tight budgets was something they all had deeply internalized and a mode it took some effort to shed. But, in this instance, as long as the resources existed, they could spend them.

"Then we launch everything we've got, make sure it's all locked into orbit, and then assemble everything in space. We don't need to spend much time discussing a number, really. We have a minimum, and that's all we need. If we're able to launch enough modules for a population of two hundred, then we do that. If we're able to get a population of a thousand, then we do that. My view is that we get as many as possible up there. That would make the population more versatile, able to stand losses, give them more of a chance to develop immunity to diseases, and so on. Then it would simply be a matter of calculating how many modules we can build and get up to orbit in time." He paused then, looking around at the others.

"What do you say, folks? We all know there will be engineering and production difficulties, but this is the way to do it, right?" Some nodded fiercely, obviously agreeing, while others, mostly the engineers, seemed skeptical. The discussion that followed was mostly too technical for Ramon to follow, but he gradually found that he agreed with the grizzled old engineer, even though some of the others pointed out that building a starship even for a population of a hundred people was a daunting task that shouldn't be complicated further with the possibility of several hundred additional passengers. It still stood to reason that the limit of what was possible wasn't really the size of the ship, but the time they had at their disposal and the number of launches possible.

The meeting continued, with hours upon hours of discussion and checking all the facts they needed for making a halfway-qualified decision. They had to determine what each launch would entail in terms of routines and checks, and while allowing for setbacks, they also discussed what could be done to speed up the launch schedules, as they realistically would in a situation where quantity meant more than the possible risks involved in each individual launch. For hours this went on, until finally they came up with a number. Havelar, who during most of the day had been unusually quiet, now took charge.

"So we have a number. Sixteen hundred people. Now, I'd like to do some math with you all, to show you what that really means. I'm a business man, you know, so running numbers is something I can do." That brought smiles and chuckles as Havelar brought up an old-fashioned drawing board so that everyone could see.

"Sixteen hundred people. In such a population, we could afford to bring some who won't bear children, but would bring skills and expertise. Hopefully we'll be able to have a decent reproduction rate, meaning that the population would double every forty years or so. That's close to the reproduction rate they had in mainly agricultural, developing nations in the twentieth century. Although it may be a little high, with the proper incentives, such as more food on the table and more people to care for each other, and with land to develop, it may not be far from what we can expect.

"Sixteen hundred people." He mused at the number he'd written in red capitals on the board.

"Doesn't seem like much of a population for an entire world, now, does it? But the key here is exponential growth. Population growth could be compared to compound interest, and we all know the power of that, don't we? Hell, I've made a living on that; I know how powerful that can be. So what kind of growth are we talking about here?" He started scribbling on the board, numbers of births per family, average life span for humans, numbers upon numbers.

"In 120 years, we're talking about 12,800 people. Still not a lot, but again, this is exponential growth. More people are added than we take away from the equation. In 200 years, we'd have 51,200 people, and in 300 years, we're talking more than 300,000 people. Add another hundred years, and there will be a million people on the new world. Isn't that something?" Ramon was stunned. Of course, as a businessman, he did these same kinds of calculations every day, he just hadn't thought about the fact that the same principles would apply here as well. What we're doing here will actually give mankind a second chance, he thought. By saving a population of sixteen hundred, they could have a million people alive within four hundred years of landing on the new world. It was a staggering number, and suddenly Ramon felt something he hadn't felt much of since that meeting when they were told what would happen to Earth. Now he felt exhilarated and eager. Ramon realized that at this very moment he had just started believing there was still hope, after all. By God, if they could just find somewhere to settle, they could actually do this!

August 2073 ~ Near Roanoke, Virginia

It was late August. In Virginia's humid summer air and sunny days, people usually took to the shade by day, coming out in the afternoons and evenings. Sitting on the terrace outside his friend's cabin, Trevor Hayes could only marvel at the view. The sun was setting and cast a red-orange light that gave the lake a glow, as if the entire lake was on fire. It was truly magnificent. Mark came out and sat beside him, handing him a can of beer, fresh from the cooler.

"What do you think?" he said. "Like the view? Spent a fortune on it. Thought it would be worth it."

Of course, they both knew it would come to an end. Mark Novak was one of the scientists brought in to work on Project Exodus. For the last few years, he'd been involved in medical research on how to sustain lower body temperatures to levels that halted metabolism. They had found that it would be entirely possible to sustain life for years, and their research had shown one of the side effects to be that the aging processes went into an almost dormant state. Aging wasn't completely halted, but so far they were able to slow it by a factor of about one hundred. Originally this had been part of an experimental study to optimize conditions for prolonged surgery, but it had always been thought that "cryo-sleep" would be quite similar to this. Now it seemed the need had arisen for just that kind of expertise, with star flight suddenly no longer a remote possibility but a requirement for the survival of the human race.

"So what happened to that fiancée of yours?" Trevor said, and grinned; he knew Mark had a history of being quite a womanizer. Mark shrugged and faked an innocent look on his face.

"Ah, she left. I have no idea why, although I doubt she sees eye to eye with her sister anymore, if you know what I mean." He winked, and Trevor burst out laughing. He hadn't seen his friend more than maybe once a year or so since they'd gone their separate ways after high school. Mark had gone to Duke University and Trevor went to Harvard. But they stayed in touch, sporadically, even though it was difficult as they were both busy and ambitious. And here they were, working on the same project, knowing what few others did. Mark looked out at the lake, and he seemed to have something on his mind.

"What's up, buddy?" Mark shook his head, which made Trevor even more certain that there was something bothering him.

"Come on, man, I know there's something." Mark didn't answer. He got a different look on his face, sort of distant, but with a touch of anger at something. He still didn't say anything as he got to his feet and went to get them both another beer. In the distance, he heard a car, and after a few seconds, he could hear it coming closer. Then, just as Trevor heard the car pull to a stop, Mark came back carrying three cans of beer.

"There's someone I'd like you to meet. His name is Thatcher. I just heard his car; he'll be here in a sec." A few moments later, a man in his fifties came around the house and greeted Mark as an old friend, then gave Trevor a firm handshake as he introduced himself.

"I'm Richard Thatcher," he said with a smile. "And I know who you are." Trevor didn't know what to say, so he laughed politely. Mark got another chair, and they all sat down. Thatcher had some kind of intensity about him, and it made Trevor a bit uneasy. Who is this man? he wondered.

"Mark here said you are the one to talk to," Thatcher smiled.

"About what?" Trevor said quizzically.

"About Exodus." Trevor felt a shiver. As national security advisor, he had a list of the names of every single person involved, and no Thatcher was on that list. His eyes narrowed, and he turned toward his friend.

"Mark, you are aware that telling …" Mark shook his head, interrupting him.

"I never told anyone, I swear. But he knows everything." Thatcher still smiled.

"Don't worry, Trevor," he said. "I'm here because I think you are a good man, and being a friend of Mark's only confirms that belief. Since you probably can't speak about this, why don't you let me sum up what I've learned so far?" Thatcher took a deep swallow from his can, and his smile widened.

"All right. Within three years, we'll be able to see Devastator with the naked eye. Have you thought about what that means? It's getting closer, so every time it comes back into view, it will be like a steadily growing star in the sky. This will go on for the next eight years or so, until impact." Trevor nodded. All this was known to him, but he didn't say anything, as it seemed Thatcher needed to show how far his knowledge went, to prove that he already knew, and that whatever Trevor said concerning the facts would be no breach of his confidentiality.

"During the last few encounters prior to impact, there will be a lot of debris falling down on Earth, as a bombardment from space, and strange weather, although I'm still not sure what they mean by that. But a lot of debris will probably settle in the upper atmosphere, causing a worldwide drop in temperatures. The effects of all that will be bad enough. But as we both know, it is impact that we really should fear. The killer impact." Thatcher stopped and spread his hands, as if saying there, now you know that I know. Trevor said nothing, so it was Mark who broke the silence.

"So, Trevor, how do you think it'll be, when the bastard hits us?" Trevor thought for a second. What could be the harm of discussing that, when Thatcher already knew the rest? He knew he shouldn't, but his curiosity for where this conversation would be going took over, so he tried to formulate an answer.

"Well, I guess there are multiple outcome possibilities, all devastating to some degree. The most probable outcome is that just a small number of people survive, by pure chance. No bunkers or shelters will do us any good here. But some will survive. To kill every living being on the planet, it would probably take the sun to explode, or the planet to disintegrate. And that won't happen." He paused, sipped his beer, and managed to smile, despite the grim topic.

"Now, humans are adaptable, more so than most of us think. Trust me, I've seen that close up more than once." Mark nodded; he knew that Trevor had seen more than most people. Not surprisingly, Thatcher seemed to know that as well.

"Those who survive such an event will be resourceful, and I don't think this will be the end of the human race. However, I do believe this will mark the end of our civilization as we know it. I don't think people have thought that far yet, but the aftermath of such an event will be a long period of sheer survival—decades, maybe centuries. Then, slowly will come a period of growth and expansion, but from almost nothing." He shook his head, thinking that this was the future they had to look forward to, if they were among the survivors. He saw that Thatcher nodded knowingly. It was obvious he'd had the same thoughts too, because before Trevor could continue, Thatcher spoke.

"In such times, knowledge that is not directly applicable to short-term survival will be deemed useless, however we think about it today. Education will be on the lowest level you can think of for a very long time, and the accumulated knowledge of human civilization will deteriorate. This will go on for a long time, until at some point the remaining population will be able to create a surplus of goods, such as food, to make trade possible again." Trevor remembered his history lessons well, and could only agree.

"Of course. Trade is the real key" he said, and Thatcher smiled.

"Yes, it is. Trade creates all kinds of specializations. And demands. Only when trade is possible will education, science, and culture regain their place in society. But by then, generations may have passed, wars may have been fought, with sticks and stones I guess, once the armories are emptied or destroyed. The lights in the sky may have changed from stars to objects of worship. Really, who knows how far this might go?" Thatcher laughed softly, although with a hint of bitterness to his voice.

"The civilization growing up from all that may not resemble ours in the least. We may not even be remembered as being real, but as a myth, as something that future human beings consider superstition! And there's always the possibility that our optimism on behalf of humanity is misplaced, and that we actually do go extinct on Earth ..."

Then Thatcher got a determined look on his face. He spoke directly to Trevor now, as Mark got up and excused himself. Then the two of them were alone on the terrace.

"So you see why we need to preserve whatever we have right now, and ship it far, far away? It may be our only chance. This civilization of ours has lost a lot of the qualities it once had, but it's still worth saving, don't you think?" Careful, Trevor thought, as he shot the older man a sharp look. Thatcher continued, undisturbed, although a twinkle in his eye gave away that he'd picked up on Trevor's reaction, and it was exactly the reaction he'd anticipated.

"Of course, a lot of the old western liberties, such as free speech, are now mostly illusory." Now Trevor subconsciously looked around to see if anyone was listening. That kind of talk was dangerous.

"But even so, the ideas still live, and we still remember societies that once actually existed, where those ideas were law. And most of them were taken for granted. We even had all that, right here, less than a century ago. That alone makes it worthwhile to try to save a small piece of our species, don't you think?" Now Trevor couldn't be silent anymore.

"What the hell is this?" he said between his teeth, as he scowled suspiciously at the man who just by being here might prove dangerous to both him and Mark.

"Who are you, and what do you want?" Then Thatcher surprised him by laughing out loud.

"I provoked you, didn't I?" he said after a few seconds. Trevor just nodded.

"All right, I understand. I know you are a true patriot, Mr. Hayes, and that you love this country deeply. What you need to understand is that so do I.

"I served in North Africa in the early days, you see. Before everything turned ugly. I've spilt blood for this country, more than once." Thatcher stared at the lake, a shimmering black now that the sun had set.

"I am as much a patriot as you are, Mr. Hayes. But when I joined the army, I swore an oath to protect and defend the Constitution. I sincerely believe that the Constitution was one of the finest texts ever written. And it wasn't just words either; every single sentence held a deep meaning, and showed us what this country should be all about."

Was. Trevor began to suspect where he was headed, and although he'd occasionally had these same thoughts himself, he knew that was a path that led to treason.

"You think I'm talking about treason here, don't you?" Trevor started at Thatcher's words. It was as if he could read his mind. The mysterious man was always a step ahead of his thoughts.

"I know you think that, you don't have to say it. But I'm not. Although I do think treason was committed when they revised the Constitution, especially when they changed the first amendment." Trevor didn't have an answer to that.

"You know, when they send those people away to some distant planet, they will try to create a copy of this society. President Andrews's society. My guess is that they will make sure the colony is set up with people like Havelar, or someone like him, in charge. Maybe even Shaw. True believers. With guns to back them up." Trevor knew there had been discussions on how to make sure the colony would be safeguarded from dissidents and subversive ideas. He had taken part in those discussions, but he'd been more concerned with the security around the selection and launch facilities, and of course the production facilities where spaceship parts would be assembled. Not to mention how to avoid terrorists getting their hands on the materials that would be used for construction of the starship, many of which could be used for making weapons of mass destruction.

"In a small population such as that one, the result will be tyranny. You see, I'm not advocating anything like overthrowing President Andrews and his regime. I'm more concerned about the future, and sad to say, that future won't be here. No, I'm talking about making sure the colony doesn't turn out the way this country has been going since Holloway." Thatcher got up and stretched his back. None of them said anything for a moment, and Trevor thought hard about what he had just heard. President Holloway had started the slow descent, with his so-called reforms, such as the financial reforms. In retrospect, these reforms had built a foundation on which President Andrews later had been able to establish structures that placed all power in the hands of a few, with no checks and balances left to speak of: an impotent congress and a subservient judiciary; a press owned by a business elite surrounding the President; and mega-corporations that were deeply intertwined in a government that made every critic turn silent or disappear. Trevor sat in the middle of it all, and knew exactly what Thatcher was speaking of. He hesitated for a moment, before speaking, choosing his words carefully.

"So what is it you want, really?"

"I want them to have what we wasted. Freedom, to read what they want, and speak whatever is on their minds. To be the masters of their own destiny, not slaves to the will of a few. I want the true Constitution to come back to life. It cannot be done here. Not anymore. It would only destroy us in these few years that we have left. But there is a new world out there somewhere, and maybe this is a chance to start over. Maybe we don't have to repeat the mistakes of the past." He smiled again, and then offered his hand to Trevor. Trevor hesitated, and then took it slowly.

"I'll be in touch," Thatcher said. Trevor stared after him, while confusing thoughts raced through his mind.

The phone rang at almost exactly nine thirty, on a Wednesday evening, while Ohio Senator Joe Buchanan was having a late dinner with his wife in their home. He didn't want to interrupt the meal, so he decided to ignore the call, and let it ring until it stopped. He didn't give it a second thought, and resumed his conversation with his wife, Cecilia. Then it rang again, and this time it didn't stop. Cecilia smiled fondly, and motioned for him to take it.

"Come on, Joe, I know you're wondering who it is. Just take it and be done with it." A little annoyed at the caller, he got up and walked over to the sideboard, where he kept his phone. The number was hidden, but since he'd already gotten up, he decided to take the call anyway. He took his phone into his study and closed the door.

"Yes," he said, waiting for the caller to identify himself.

"Senator," the voice on the other end answered. It sounded vaguely familiar to him, but he couldn't quite place it. So, he figured it had to be someone he knew from way back.

"You may not remember me, but we worked together on the Stephenson bill, I guess it's been about twenty years ago now ... My name is Richard Thatcher. I was on the team of the late Senator Williamson back then." Joe had to think hard for a second before it dawned upon him.

"Yes, that's right. I believe I heard your name mentioned a couple of years ago, though I can't remember the occasion; you're with the Energy Committee now, aren't you? Still working behind the scenes?"

"Well, I was for a while, before I started working for the Presidential Alternative Energy Initiative." The PAEI had been former president Holloway's green alibi, and had gotten a lot of support from environmentalist groups, although those within the inner circle and the PAEI managers knew it had nothing to do with environmentalism. It was yet another security measure, as Holloway had been just as obsessed with security as the current president. Of course, it did have an effect upon the dependency of fossil fuels, which was necessary, because the available sources were quickly dwindling, but there were secrets within secrets, and some suspected the ultimate goal was to develop entirely new classes of weapons, the kinds one could only find in fiction.

"So, Mr. Thatcher, I remember you, and we did work together when we were both young men. What is it that you want from me now?" That was the usual Joe Buchanan; no time for bullshit, straight to the point, with only the minimum of niceties.

"I need to know that you haven't changed your views on the things we spoke of that evening, when we had gotten the bill passed, after dinner." Joe knew exactly what Thatcher was talking about. He hadn't talked about it since Seattle, though; it was not safe anymore. That kind of talk could both end his career and possibly put him behind bars, and he had no desire for either. Even so, his views in private had never changed.

"I remember," he said, not wanting to reveal anything more on the phone. These days, you never knew whether your phone was tapped; the government could do that, and regularly did, and it was legal; they didn't even need a warrant or due cause.

"Good. That's very good to hear," Thatcher said, and Joe could hear him breathe out, relaxing a bit more.

"I need to talk to you. That's all I can say for now, but you actually need to talk to me as well." Buchanan wondered if that was really the case, but his curiosity had already taken over, so he agreed.

"All right, when and where?" He could hear Thatcher's low chuckle, and then his reply puzzled him.

"Good-bye for now, I'll be in touch." Then he hung up the phone. The senator just stood there for a second, confused as to what just happened. The end of the conversation did nothing to relieve his curiosity, so he was deep in thought when he returned to the dinner table. His wife could easily see he was distracted.

"Who was that, dear? What is it?" Joe just shook his head and waved it all away.

"Just some old coworker. Seems they want to have some kind of reunion. He should know I don't have time for such things." He shrugged, while Cecilia laughed softly, handing him a cruet of warm gravy to revive his meal, which had turned cold.

"Well, if you decide to go, I want to go too. We never go out just for fun anymore. It's all politics these days. Maybe it would do us some good." The senator nodded, while lost in thought. He remembered that conversation all those years ago, all too vividly. When they happened to touch upon the proposed revisions to the Constitution, and what that would mean. The things he'd said, and later regretted. Not because he didn't mean those things, but because, even back then, they were such dangerous thoughts, to himself and everyone around him. The political climate had already turned, and his ideas of preserving the Constitution rather than revising it had already been deemed reactionary, and contrary to the development of a safe and secure society, free from the threat of terrorism and subversive elements. Now, he instinctively knew that what he was getting himself into would be very dangerous, so why was he all excited about it?

The next morning, as he was getting ready for work, his tablet beeped twice, and he looked at the new message. It was from a hidden sender, and there were just two words: "Sakura Noon." He chuckled softly. To most people the message would be cryptic, but to him it made perfect sense: location and time. Sakura had been a Sushi bar, although it hadn't existed for over ten years. These days it was a rundown catering business. The time was a bit more elegant, as there had been a Japanese Noon, sort of a happy hour, with lower prices on everything. Japanese Noon would be at ten in the evening here. He deleted the message, kissed Cecilia good-bye, and went out to his car.

Winter was coming. It was one of those evenings when you could just smell it in the air. It was getting chilly fast, and Joe had put on his dark blue coat and a green scarf to keep warm. He could see the place was closed, although there was a dim light in one of the windows, as if it came from a back room. The door was open, so he entered slowly. He'd been right about the light, it came from the kitchen. A voice suddenly spoke quietly from the darkness to his right, startling him just a little.

"You came." It was Thatcher, and when he stepped a little closer, Joe could see a well-dressed man in his early fifties, with a trimmed beard, gray hair, and just a hint of a potbelly. He motioned for Joe to follow him, and they entered the lit kitchen, where another man and a woman waited. The woman seemed stern and had a suspicious look about her; her glasses and her hair, pulled back from her face with a hairpin, emphasized the impression. The man, in his early thirties, with a typical military bearing and haircut to match, wearing a dark sweater and jeans, nodded curtly to him. Thatcher did the introductions.

"Senator Buchanan, this is Dr. Amanda Shearing, of JPL at CalTech, and Air Force Lieutenant Deacon Frost." They all shook hands and Joe coughed.

"Well … I'm not sure what to make of this. Honestly, Richard, what is this all about?" Thatcher sat down on one of the chairs around a rickety table, took out a file folder, and spread his notes out. The paper seemed a little old fashioned to Joe, but then again, there would be no risk of electronic surveillance picking it up either.

"The information I have here … I could go to jail for this, and so could all of you here in this room. Just for being here. Or worse, I guess, if they knew what I have in mind. But alas, that is less of a concern to me now than it has ever been, because in a few years it won't matter. However, if this meeting goes well, there is still hope. Sort of … Please sit down, Senator, all of you. Dr. Shearing, why don't you brief the good senator?" The woman hesitated, and Buchanan felt her eyes staring into him, as if she could see every doubt he had.

"I'm still not sure we can trust …" Thatcher cut her off.

"Senator Buchanan is to be trusted. He is a good man, and I vouch for him. Continue, please. He needs to know." Dr. Shearing shook her head slowly, then rose as she picked up one of Thatcher's files and pushed it over to the senator.

"Hmm, well, I guess we don't have a choice in the matter." She took a deep breath, and managed something that was meant to be a smile.

"I guess we all get somewhat paranoid, and with good reason. But I'll trust you, Senator. What I am about to tell you is something that's being kept even from many of the people actually working on it, and if no one does anything about it, one tragedy will only be succeeded by another."

"Okay. It all started when Devastator was first discovered, more than two years ago …" And then she told him everything.

When Dr. Shearing finally sat down, Joe was pale and speechless. He didn't say anything for a minute, and the others let him digest the news. Hearing about what was likely to be the end of human civilization on Earth, from a professor who didn't strike him as a lunatic, made him shake a little. And he knew in his heart what the president's plan would mean. There would be no critical voices, no opposition to the totalitarian and restrictive ways that had evolved through the years following the Seattle incident. What would that do to the chances of survival for those who would live? And moreover, what would it mean to the society they would create, should they ever reach their destination?

"This is a heavy burden, knowing these things …" he said quietly. "I wish I could do something, but I'm truly lost here." He closed his eyes for a moment to think.

"I'm usually well informed, as well as anyone I guess." Joe had been a congressman for years, before taking a seat in the Senate, which after the second reforms had turned out to be one of the last entities where the president had to bargain and horse trade in order to make policy. Of course, the executive usually won, but even the power of stalling and renegotiation was something exclusive to the Senate these days.

"He needs me too much to cut me off completely, or at least that's what I thought. But I was kept in the dark about this, and I think that would demonstrate how powerless I am here." Thatcher shook his head, and smiled wryly.

"On the contrary, it just demonstrates that you are not one of his cronies, and I'd say that's a good thing. You know, there is a reason I called you, and it's not just to give you bad news. We mean to change the game, and I believe we have the means to do so." Joe looked quizzically at him, while Thatcher paused for a moment. Then he turned toward the younger man.

"Lieutenant Frost here comes from a very prominent family in Houston, Texas."

"Black gold, old fossils, also known as oil," Frost grimaced.

"Yes, oil money from back in the early nineteenth," Thatcher continued. Money that was used to finance the campaigns of both Holloway and Andrews.

"Money that got me into the Academy," Frost said quietly. Thatcher shook his head and dismissed his comment with a hand.

"I don't think so, Deacon. But yes, there is corruption at work, and we mean to use it to our advantage." He turned back toward Joe and picked up another file, scanned it for a moment, and then explained.

"Lieutenant Frost has been selected for a very special mission out west. He hasn't been told what it is, but I happen to know that in six months the first candidates for an undisclosed space mission will start gathering in an old air force base in Arizona, and it seems our young lieutenant's destination is that very same place. Now, that could mean anything, if it wasn't for his prior assignments, his résumé, so to speak. Since graduation from the Air Force Academy,

Lieutenant Frost has been an instructor at the Advanced Tactical School, which turns out most of the scramjet pilots. To understand the significance of this, you need to understand that most instructors at ATS are seasoned veterans, scramjet-certified pilots themselves. What I mean to say is, no offense Deacon, but your comment on money getting you into AFA is a load of crap. You've distinguished yourself too much for that to be true. No, to be selected for such an assignment without all that experience, you have to be extraordinary.

"When we send a starship into space carrying the hope of mankind, there will be a rigorous selection of candidates. Lieutenant Frost's specialty is assessing the capabilities of others for extreme conditions, for coping with the unexpected and making do with the resources at hand. It's a perfect match of the capabilities needed to create a viable colony off-Earth, and the lieutenant is an expert at it himself, as well as assessing it in others. My guess is that he will be on the team of instructors that will also be responsible for the selection of candidates."

"All right," Joe interrupted. "I can see where you're going here. Lieutenant Frost will be able to influence the selection of the candidates, and that's all very well. I like the idea of having someone carrying the torch when the rest of us are gone. But that's already in play, and I still don't know how I fit into the picture." Thatcher leaned forward on the table and stared intently at him.

"Senator, Lieutenant Frost's efforts will be of utmost importance. The crew and passengers of the starship will shape the future of our species. There may be others that will try to save some of their population, most notably the Chinese and the Indians, but we have no way of knowing what that will amount to. So, as far as we know, the ones gathering out in Arizona six months from now will be the most important people on the planet.

"If you decide to help us, Senator, you will play an important role, and your actions will be crucial to the outcome of this. You need to gain President Andrews's trust. He already knows that you don't agree on certain parts of his politics, but since you've been careful, he doesn't know what kind of rebel you really are." That last comment was said with a wry grin.

"You do have his ear, at least to a certain degree. Now use that. Develop a trust with the man; influence him as much as possible. There are issues that can significantly alter the chances of actually preserving something of what this country once was. Such as whether or not to accept certain of the more prominent candidates, such as leading scientists with views that differ from the mainstream, the choice of commander for the mission, whether there will be a large security or military contingent, or whether to allow the rich to buy passes with donations. We actually have a good number of supporters in that group, believe it or not. There are more of us than you could possibly know, Senator, and some are in a position to really make a difference. As for selection, if we get a good number of people on board that are able and willing to think for themselves, there will be hope. While Lieutenant Frost works on the selection of individuals, you may be able to influence selection policy. We may even have a plan that would place us on the inside of the loop, to practically take over the entire project—quietly of course. That plan involves you. And that, Senator, will be your true legacy when the time comes to start all over on a new world."

Chapter 5

April 2074 ~ Somewhere in Arizona

The hangar was open on one side, facing east toward the airfield. The morning sun still sat low on the horizon and lit the interior where a group of people, obviously figures of authority, a few uniformed, most civilians, was gathered on a raised podium. As Maria Solis entered the hangar, a man in a dark suit stepped forward to the microphone, tapped it lightly, and started speaking.

"Everybody, come closer. You all need to hear this." There were a couple of hundred gathered in front of the podium, and they all stepped forward a bit. Maria stayed back, but followed. A blonde girl her age smiled at her.

"Hey," the girl whispered. "You know what this is all about?" Maria shook her head, and the girl continued.

"My high school principal came and took me out of class just the other day. He said he didn't know anything, but he had orders to get me to the airport as soon as possible. Guess it's something special, with all the suits up there." She grinned with the whitest smile Maria had ever seen.

"I'm Geena, by the way."

"Maria here," she said. Then they quieted down as the man began speaking again.

"I'm Daniel Shaw, director of the Exodus Project, as it is known. Actually, it's more of a program, with many projects going on simultaneously, but somebody, somewhere decided to call it a project, so what the heck. The details of the project will be revealed to you gradually as it evolves, but I'm here today to welcome you all. You are to be part of a selection process for a space mission." There were gasps and surprised whispers that were quickly subdued by Shaw's raised hand.

"Hear me out, please." He paused and looked out over the audience.

"Now, to most of you the idea of a space mission will sound absurd. You are lawyers, business people, soldiers, librarians, high school students, dentists, and so on. That will all be explained to you later. But let me tell you this. In two weeks there will be about ten thousand others, give or take, with just as diverse backgrounds, gathered on this site. All of you will have been chosen for some reason, and there will be others with similar backgrounds as yours." Maria looked around her, and now she saw others that looked like they could be in high school too. She wondered what would be the reason for taking kids out of school like this. She would miss so many classes; there had to be something really serious going on.

"At first you will be placed among others like yourselves, so that the instructors can compare you more easily. In the time to come, some will drop out and some will be cut from the process. You will be taught a variety of subjects, and you will be given tasks to complete, alone and in groups. And at all times there will be instructors around who will assess your performance. I cannot say how long you will be here, or how many will make it in the end." He paused, looked down at his notes, and bit his lip. He spoke clearly and authoritatively, but Maria thought he looked nervous as he fiddled with his papers.

"Some of you will think this is a load of crap, and I assure you it is not. This is about as serious as it gets, and although I'm not at liberty to reveal any details to you, all I can say is that you have been given an opportunity most people could only dream about. And when you know the whole truth of this, you will know why you must make every effort, use every skill you have, and learn as much as you can. Thank you for your attention, and good luck to all of you." He turned and walked back to the others, and then walked down from the podium and through a door in the back. A bald, mustached man in uniform took his place, turned off the microphone, and just stood there for a second. Then he spoke, in a gruff voice, loud and clear.

"Listen up," he called out.

"I'm Colonel Harris, and I'm in charge of all day-to-day operations at this site. You will see me and hear me, but you will not speak to me unless spoken to. Are we clear?" He seemed to look right at her for a second, even though she stood as far back as she could get, and thought she looked as anonymous as anyone. He pointed to the southern end of the hangar.

"On that wall there are lists with all your names on them, in alphabetical order. To the right of your name you will find a number. That is the number of your group. You will also find a capital letter after your number. That is the building where you will be staying. Throughout this compound there are a number of buildings, so you will also be given a map of the area. Now, when you get to where your group will stay, get to know each other well. You will need to. As the director told you, you will have about two weeks until everybody has arrived, so there is plenty of time for that." He paused for a moment, then gave the audience that see-through-them stare again.

"Now, I could wish you good luck, as the director did. But my task here is to make sure we get the very best of you, and that everyone else is weeded out, so I'm not going to wish you any luck at all. What I wish is for everyone to do their best, pay attention, learn, and then perform. That's it. And then, if you do that, you might have a chance to stand out, and get through the selection process. Those of you who do that will be on my final list, and that's really all you should wish for." Then, surprisingly, he smiled broadly, as if he'd said something funny.

"Welcome to Project Exodus."

May 2074 ~ Los Angeles, California

The Consortium had been through this discussion many times already, but the time had come to make a decision. Out west, the selection of candidates for the starship had already begun, construction of hab and cargo modules were already under way, and the scientists were already conducting human testing of cryo techniques that would be used during interstellar flight. It was time to decide on the means of propulsion, how to get from Earth orbit to the new world. They were sitting in a conference room in the Pasadena offices of JPL, and on the furthest wall there was a screen where President Andrews, the science advisor, and George Havelar followed the discussion from their seats in the White House, and sometimes interjected comments or questions. Dr. Amanda Shearing of JPL started by summing up the discussion so far.

"Back in the early days of space flight, there were a few options, but none was sufficient for reasonable interstellar flight. Chemical propulsion could theoretically get a starship from Earth to Alpha Centauri, just 4.3 light years away, which is closer than any other star system, in a little less than eight millennia." She paused, grinning wryly.

"Which, of course, would be out of the question. With nuclear fission, the time would be reduced drastically. In principle, with nuclear fission we could generate an exhaust velocity of 4 percent of light speed, and using a gravity assist, such as that of Jupiter or the sun, we would be able to achieve 8 percent of light speed. That would enable the journey to Alpha Centauri to take fifty-four years, although one critical factor needs to be accounted for: deceleration. Using nuclear fission for deceleration would increase transit time to 108 years. Of course, with a magnetic sail for deceleration, which is certainly doable, we would be able to utilize the entire exhaust velocity for acceleration, so 8 percent is probably the number to keep in mind here. But remember that these speed estimates are theoretical possibilities. In the real world, we'd probably not be able to achieve much more than 2 or 3 percent of light speed with fission.

"Also, let's not forget that it's unlikely that we're going to find the planet we seek at the shortest possible distance. My guess is that we'll have to be looking at the stars further out, such as Gliese 581, at a little more than twenty light years away, or 55 Cancri, which is about forty-one light years away. Not much further though. I guess there will be a limit somewhere around fifty to eighty light years away though, and we'll plan accordingly. But even so, at twenty light years, fission is also impractical." They all nodded; they'd been through this before, so this first session was mainly to bring their White House attendees up to speed, although Ramon silently felt better getting the condensed facts this way, since sometimes these discussions seemed to go way over his head. Now, having patiently presented the pros and cons of the impractical options, Dr. Shearing turned to the more realistic options as to the prospect of being able to bring the starship from A to B.

"Now, a deuterium and helium-3 fusion rocket may be able to produce an exhaust velocity of 5 percent of light speed. With gravity assist and efficient engineering, this could be increased to 10 percent. That would give us a transit time to Alpha Centauri of approximately forty-three years, or eighty-six years if we also use this method for deceleration. For distances of twenty light years or more, it's still a bit on the slow side, but the technology is within reach. It can be done.

"Another option is solar sails. This was already in the works when NASA was disbanded, and the Europeans have already used solar sails for unmanned probes for more than a decade. Although the purely solar-powered sails the Europeans are using are too slow for star flight, with a theoretical maximum speed of little more than 1 percent of light speed, we could increase the speed dramatically by giving the sails a decent push. What we need then is a high-energy laser lens. We're talking about a 250-meter-wide lens, a huge engineering project by itself, but possible, given the resources we're willing to spend here. But the energy consumption is dramatic. The power needed would be more than 25 percent of the entire world's energy consumption for about four months, fission probably. It is a practical issue, really. The lens would have to be constructed in space, and in addition to the fission-powered laser, it would consist of a chemical rocket that would push it out of Earth orbit, and then trail the starship. Then it would point the laser at the starship's sail for four months, until the starship reached a cruise velocity of about 25 percent of light speed. This option would be devastating to our world economy, and it's not something that would have been considered under normal circumstances. But this is hardly a normal circumstance now, is it?"

"I'm sorry to interrupt, but I have some serious doubts that such a project could be finished on time." That was Eric Sloan, also of JPL, speaking. Throughout the previous meetings, he'd continuously referred to the engineering issues, and while admitting that solar sails seemed the best option when speed was concerned, his insight into low earth orbit engineering and its difficulties led him to oppose the addition of a high-energy laser lens.

"I just don't see how we're going to have the manpower for two immense construction projects at the same time. Remember, we only have about five to seven years to do this. A smaller laser, yes, that could be possible, but the sheer size we're talking about here simply demands more time. And that's time we don't have. If we had enough qualified construction personnel, it would be possible, but we don't have the time to train these people, and the energy still has to be produced, which is an immense challenge. And let's not forget the solar sails themselves. The construction of such micro-thin materials would also have to be done in space, and that's after we develop a new way of constructing them. The European model would be useless for interstellar travel, and again the scarce resource is time. So in my view, we should go for simpler, meaning a slower starship and longer transit time."

"So what do you think we should do?" the president asked. Sloan thought for a moment before he replied.

"I believe fusion is our best option, since technology is already in place, or close enough. The

Deuterium and Helium-3 fusion rocket will give us 10 percent of light speed, and I simply cannot see any other option that will be possible, given the time at our disposal. The solar sail option has the upside of giving us great speed, if it could be finished in time, if all R&D is successful, and if we can get the power needed. That's a lot of ifs, and the consequences of even a small setback could topple the entire project. So if I'm to have a say in this, I'd go for fusion." Several of the others nodded, and even Dr. Shearing seemed to agree. Ramon could certainly see the advantages of solar sails, but Dr. Sloan did have a point. There were too many what-ifs. He'd rather place his bet on a starship that would be using a simpler technology, even though it meant sacrificing speed. It was then that Dr. Grant, having said nothing since the meeting started, decided to join in the conversation. He leaned forward and spoke, while at the same time checking something on his tablet.

"I might have something here, just a second … Damn, there's too little openness in the world …" he muttered to himself, earning sideways glances from some of the others.

"It seems there was an interesting discovery by ESA a while back … It's been kept secret, probably due to some scientists wanting to make sure they've got the facts straight.

Damn fools, still more concerned about their publications than sharing knowledge … It's a friend of mine at ESA, saying that some of his colleagues found something about 0.3 light years out. Wait …" He then typed something on his tablet, waited for a few seconds, eyes widening when he got the reply. A wide grin spread across his face.

"He says that they finally found definite proof of the existence of Nemesis."

"What's Nemesis?" the president asked, furrowing his brows, and tightening his lips at the new information that seemed to come out of nowhere.

"Well, it's a star, sort of," Grant replied, smiling as he laid his tablet down on the table. "There is a theory that the mass extinctions we've seen in the past, such as the dinosaurs, were caused by comets released from their relatively stable orbits out in the Oort Cloud by the gravitational influence of a star locked in an orbit that brings it as close to the sun as 0.1 light years every twenty-six million years. Now, the supporting evidence for this theory is the mass extinctions themselves, of course, but also the fact that there are gravitational forces out there that cannot be accounted for, and that suggests that currently undetected objects may actually exist in near solar space." He checked his tablet again, then raised his eyebrows, and smiled knowingly.

"Seems the theory was wrong on a few important points though, which is to our advantage. The orbit is a lot closer than first assumed, although it never gets any closer than 0.1 light years .... Hmm, yes. All right, this is it. Nemesis is a brown dwarf. No wonder we haven't detected it before, I'm surprised they even managed to find it. Brown dwarves are proto stars that never ignited, so they are very hard to detect because they emit very little heat and light. So ... Ah ... Nemesis, with a mass twenty times that of Jupiter, is locked in an orbit that takes about thirteen million years to circle the sun, and that explains the mass extinctions. Seems it only releases the devastating comets every other round, for some reason. At its aphelion, meaning its furthest distance from the sun, it will be about 1.8 light years away, while its perihelion, that is the closest it gets, is located at 0.11 light years from the sun. Its current position is 0.3 light years out, and it will stay at that approximate distance a long time after the starship has passed." He looked up from his tablet again, grinning from ear to ear, and from the expression on Sloan's face, he had also seen what this meant. Ramon was fascinated, although he still didn't see the relevance of all this.

Grant shook his head, still smiling, and now Shearing also chimed in.

"That opens up a whole new range of options for us, don't you think?" She looked at Sloan, who was punching at his own tablet like crazy, crunching the numbers. He nodded fiercely.

"This is fantastic. You know, using the Deuterium and Helium-3 fusion rocket, with a maximum gravity assisted velocity of 10 percent of light speed it would take us three years to reach Nemesis, ignoring acceleration time. With acceleration and gravity assist from the sun, we're talking five to six years. I'll have to do the math on that ... Now, with a second gravity assist from Nemesis, we can easily obtain a speed of 25 to 35 percent of light speed. That's just ... staggering ..."

"He he, the timing couldn't have been better, right?" Grant said.

"Say, six years to Nemesis, then a gravity assist that gives us a little more than 25 percent of light speed, sixteen years to Alpha Centauri, then three years of braking. We're talking twenty-five years here. And that's a conservative estimate." Dr. Shearing, as the authority on the issue, then spoke directly to the president.

"Of course, we need to check all the facts, and make sure there is absolutely no possibility that the Europeans have made a mistake. Barring that, I'd say we have a recommendation." The president just nodded, with a satisfied expression on his face. Havelar, always onto the practical details, looked up at the scientist.

"How soon before you can be absolutely certain? We need to get production started, whatever decision we come to." Shearing, skeptical toward Havelar's involvement, as she'd voiced, although carefully, several times, looked at Grant, who answered.

"Give us three weeks. Usually we'd need more, a lot more, but it seems the Europeans have been onto this for years, so it should be just a matter of talking to them and looking at the figures ourselves. Then we'll be ready."

Chapter 6

July 2076 ~ Sonora, Arizona

They were somewhere in the Sonora desert. Captain Tina Hammer felt weak, her throat parched, head throbbing, legs resisting her every movement. Whoever said black people don't get sunburned was an idiot. Her face showed a deep red from sunburn, and there were signs of blisters developing on her nearly shaven head. She didn't sweat anymore, even in the sweltering heat and being physically exhausted from days of trekking across the desert; she was too dehydrated. Her companions, Navy ensigns Dean Johnson and Kim Leffard and Army Lieutenant Henry Carroll, were still hanging on by sheer willpower, although Leffard was now slowing them down due to a sprained ankle.

"You should go on. I'll catch up," Kim said, while breathing heavily. "I just need a breather; you guys won't get far without me anyways!" She was about the toughest woman Hammer had ever known, but sprained ankle or no, she now looked like she'd spent the last of her strength. Henry slumped down beside her, coughing heavily.

"Yeah right, and let you off that easily, eh?" He tried to pry off his right boot, but lost his balance, even sitting.

Then he managed to slowly take it off, and saw that blood had seeped through his socks.

"I guess we're both fucked good and hard now, Leffard. I don't think I'll be able to walk on this again for a while." He shook his head.

"So damn close ... It must be ..." He took a pebble and put it in his mouth, an old trick. After a couple of seconds he spit it out again.

"Humph, never worked," Henry continued. "Whoever made that one up never spent a week in the desert." He licked his cracked lips, and grimaced. Then he lay back and closed his eyes.

Tina held up her hand and squinted to the east. They'd walked quite a ways since being dumped out of the chopper a few nights back, blindfolded and with only a couple of water bottles to share. She had no idea how far they had come, but the first few days they had walked a good twelve hours, daytime, before deciding it would be better to walk by night and rest while the sun was at its highest. That worked for another couple of days. After that, things had moved more slowly. Fatigue, blisters, hunger, and eventually thirst had slowly taken their toll. They had no idea how long they had to go, or whether they would be picked up if they decided they'd had it. Tina was deeply concerned. As the senior officer, she was in charge, and although she suspected they were being monitored somehow, in the back of her mind she worried that they were too far off the grid. Or that the instructors had dropped them out here to see how many would survive, and that losses were expected. She'd seen it before, and the situation was definitely extreme; in fact, you couldn't get more extreme than this. It could be that this was the kind of situation where such extreme training and selection were deemed necessary. She rose to her feet, deciding such thinking was useless, and reached out for Kim's hand.

"Let's go. It can't be far now. And if we don't get there today, I'd like to find some shade. Come on, you too, Dean. Henry, you'll just have to suck it up. You know that the pain numbs after a while. Now get that boot back on while you can. And no more of that 'carry on without me' crap, Kim." Tina put her concerns away for now; the group was her responsibility, they were her team, and by far the best she'd ever worked with, and there was no way she'd let them down. She would not show her doubts.

They reached a dried out riverbed and decided to rest for a few hours. Somehow, they were still standing, but dehydration was now becoming a real danger. If they didn't find any water soon … At least they had some shade; there were a few large scattered boulders that gave them some respite from the blinding white sun. Tina's concerns had grown steadily over the last few hours, however hard she tried to suppress them. Of the four, she was probably the one in the best shape at the moment, although she felt the pain and exhaustion in every part of her body. She knew that, unless their instructors decided to show up, or they found some source of water, which didn't seem likely now, her worst fears would come to life. She stared up at the cloudless sky, watching an eagle circling overhead, slowly, watching them, undisturbed by the human presence. Sleep evaded her, although she was so tired, oh so tired.

They had been split up into groups of twenty to twenty-five within the first weeks after arrival, and those groups seemed matched so that candidates with similar intended roles were grouped together. She'd been put in a group of experienced officers, Navy, Army, Air Force, even a couple of astronauts, which surprised her, as those were a rare breed these days. They were diverse in a lot of ways, but all had the common denominator that they were used to command on at least company level, or some equivalent. She knew other groups were similarly put together, and inferred that from each group, only one or two would be on the final list.

There had been all kinds of activities, from arctic survival training to physics projects, mechanical training, basic to intermediate surgery, military exercises of every variety; it was hard to quite see how it all made sense. At some point during the first year, she'd discussed it with a colonel whose name she couldn't remember.

"Redundancy," the colonel had explained. "What happens if you lose half your crew on final descent?"

"But you wouldn't put all your eggs in one basket," Tina had argued. "You'd split the crew according to competencies, so you'd always have someone left who could do the job."

The colonel had nodded, then scratched his cropped black hair, while chewing on some kind of nuts he had this weakness for.

"Of course, but what if … What if you had to split your crew differently? This is nothing like we're used to; you know that. What if the crew had to be split according to demographics? What if you had to make sure there were enough men and enough women on each landing craft to be able to breed? What if you had to choose between sick and healthy? What if not half, but most of the crew were wiped out by some freak accident?" It was probably at some point during that conversation that Tina really began to understand the nature of what this mission was all about. Of course, it wasn't until the news about Devastator had leaked that she'd truly fathomed the finality of it all, that this was probably humanity's only chance for survival. But it was the conversation with the colonel that had opened her eyes to the fact that this was so much more than she'd expected when she was picked for Selection. If she could only remember his name ...

The colonel had washed out during one of the weeding processes that happened at irregular intervals, just a few months after Tina's conversation with him, and she'd never seen the man again. Rumor had it the rejects were moved to detention centers so that they were unable to reveal anything, for security reasons. She wouldn't normally believe such rumors, but under the circumstances, she wouldn't rule it out. The fact was, no one really knew.

The eagle circling above seemed to be closing in on them. What does it want? Tina thought. Somehow, she was vaguely aware that she was delirious, a weird feeling, kind of what she imagined an out-of-body experience must be like.

The eagle landed and opened a door on the side of its belly. It was huge! Out of the door, little people jumped out, some in white, others in desert fatigues. A funny eagle, Tina grinned, whoever heard of an eagle with doors, and people inside. She passed out.

Tina woke slowly to murmured voices in a white, cool air-conditioned room. Ensign Johnson was standing next to another bed, where a middle-aged doctor and a tall, suited man were standing beside a sleeping Henry Carroll.

"He's been through surgery, seems his leg was worse than we thought," she heard Kim Leffard whisper quietly. "Some kind of infection. It's a wonder he made it that far. Tough bastard." Tina nodded in agreement. They were quite a team now: herself, Kim, Henry and Dean. They'd been in different groups throughout most of Selection, and had been put together as a team only six months ago. Now they were a tightly knit group, and she expected their experiences in the desert would bond them even tighter. Perhaps that was the whole purpose, she pondered.

The man in the suit turned toward her.

"Ah, it seems our pilot is back," he said, revealing a broad smile, and a hint of pride in his eyes. He was clean-shaven, with dark blond hair, and couldn't have been more than forty, although it was difficult to tell. The eyes, deep blue, seemed older, somehow.

"You, ma'am, have just made one hell of an impression. The Board has had their eyes on you for some time, and with good reason. Your team held on the longest of all, and you pulled everyone through till the end. You should be proud. I know I am."

"Proud?" Tina said weakly. She still didn't quite understand; she felt quite weak.

"Yes, damn proud. You don't know me, but I've followed you for almost two years now. I'm on the Selection Board and you, ma'am, have been one of my favorites almost from day one. And I'm also happy to see that your team is ready to start your next phase of training."

October 2076 ~ Washington, DC

Trevor Hayes was a man of few words, and his appointment four years ago as national security advisor had surprised a good number of Washington insiders. The media had also been taken by surprise, and they've been digging ever since to find background on this largely anonymous man. So far, very little had been found, except what was available from official sources. He had attended Harvard Law, and then served with the notorious Black Berets for close to ten years, before leaving the service to work for Pegasus Inc., a medium-sized company that provided security and private military services, a growing industry in the age of terror. The official file on him said he had worked in both the legal department and in several managerial and executive positions, and, although unsubstantiated, there were rumors that he was also involved in the company's more clandestine operations. Within seven years, Hayes had become a partner, which meant a more public role. He had been involved in several of the lawsuits following the growth of the industry, but somehow they had escaped the media radar, being overshadowed by larger scandals, such as the royal wedding drug scandal in England and the Louisiana governor's involvement in trafficking, which had covered the front pages for weeks. When the Supreme Court had dismissed the cases, there had been some stirring and talk of a shift in the checks and balances, assigning greater powers to the executive branch, but still Hayes had been just one of the many lawyers involved, although it was well known that he was one of the figures emerging as a leader of an industry growing steadily more entrenched with the sitting administration. And as America was evolving more and more each year into a one-party system, Trevor Hayes steadily rose in the ranks of the establishment.

And now, in the Oval Office, sitting in a lounge chair opposite from him, President Andrews absently swirled a wide glass of whiskey, while considering Trevor's latest proposal. The president hadn't touched his drink once, which, to Trevor, meant he shouldn't touch his either. The president gritted his teeth, still not meeting his eyes, obviously considering both the news he'd been given and the solution brought to him by one of his most trusted advisors. Hayes knew this very moment would either ruin his position with the president and severely damage his chances of success, or bring him a lot closer to one of his main objectives, the one he'd been working toward ever since his gradual involvement in the schemes of the charismatic and persuasive Thatcher.

"You're sure about this?" the president asked him, his mask impossible to read.

"Yes, sir."

"You want me to dump the one man that's gotten Project Exodus this far? Is that your recommendation? That I replace him with a man I'm less sure about, one that I actually, to be frank, trust less?" President Andrews was often considered a man who valued loyalty over competence. Trevor Hayes would never underestimate him that way, although he saw that the question of loyalty would matter here, as the project was the president's most important issue these days. And his only hope was that Senator Buchanan's years of political maneuvering and the way he'd become a close ally of this administration through years as a party insider would deem him loyal enough to be entrusted with this project.

"Mr. President, we both know Senator Buchanan doesn't agree with every one of your policies. But I think this only strengthens his candidacy. You know he will tell you his honest opinion, and you don't need another sycophant that only tells you what you want to hear. That could be devastating when it comes to the project. When it comes to loyalty, I'd say that having someone who's stuck with you through the years, despite occasional differences, is the kind of loyalty you'd want in a person who also needs to make tough decisions. And you don't want someone who needs to be micro managed because he's afraid of not always agreeing with you on every little detail." Hayes knew this would strike a chord with the president, since for the past few years that had become a very real difficulty, but he couldn't be sure that would be enough. The stakes were extreme at this point, and he had no way of knowing whether President Andrews would be persuaded by arguments or fall back on his tendency to demand blind loyalty from those closest to him.

The president got up from his chair, put his glass back on the table, still untouched, and walked over to the windows. He stood there for a moment, his back toward Hayes, staring out the window, where fallen leaves now covered the lawn outside. Hayes could see he was troubled, but didn't interrupt him. This was the turning point, the point where he would see whether the plan had worked, whether or not the movement would gain access to the one position of influence, except the presidency of course, where they could seriously affect the outcome of the biggest gamble of all time. If it worked, they would actually stand a chance of success. If it didn't, well, they would be back to square one, with no time to pick up the pieces.

Then the president turned.

"I trusted Mr. Shaw, you know. Apparently I didn't know him well enough. I will have him removed immediately. I have no choice in the matter; I cannot keep that perverted, sick ..." President Andrews stopped before his anger got the better of him, then walked briskly back to the table, picked up his drink, and emptied it.

"All right, Trevor, set up a meeting with Senator Buchanan first thing tomorrow. Tell him to put everything else aside. And prepare a briefing, in which he will be fully informed. He needs to know what he's getting himself into. From now on, he is to be treated as one of us."

Later, walking through the hallways of the White House, Trevor Hayes had that weird feeling that everyone he encountered could see his exhilaration, that every emotion that raced through him was clearly visible on the outside for everyone to see. Of course, that was just how he felt. After all, he was a professional, and he'd been in the cloak and dagger business for years. He knew how to put on a blank face and hide his natural, biological reactions, such as heightened heart rate and pumping adrenaline. He had succeeded. Tomorrow, Senator Joe Buchanan would be appointed by the president to manage the Exodus Project. Ironic, Hayes thought, President Andrews just gave his greatest enemies the weapons needed to destroy his legacy. He will have no idea what hit him.

January 2077 ~ Antarctica

This was said to be a learning experience; no cuts, no weeding out this time, and it did seem to be true, at least for the time being. Maria Solis knew they were somewhere in Antarctica, probably on the high plains, because of the altitude. They could feel the thin air, and while they'd been blessed with nice weather, the sun warming just a little and no wind to speak of, the hard-packed snow still felt crisp beneath her feet, and her every breath stung just a little in her lungs, even with the face mask.

"How ya doin' over there, Solis? Breckinbridge?" she heard Jeremiah Lowell call at her and her friend Sophie Breckinbridge. He was standing a bit to their left, his back bent, trying to bring life back to the snowmobile, which seemed utterly dead at the moment.

"How's it gonna be? Y'all gonna just stand there, or ya'll gonna help out? Jesse could use another pair of hands on the tent." To people who didn't know him, his Southern twang could sometimes seem faked, as he'd lose it from time to time, but Maria knew better. A professor in the Geology department at Cambridge, England, he'd somehow over time developed a curious mixture of his native accent and pretty standard Oxford English, and for some reason there was no apparent consistency to it.

She nudged Sophie with her elbow, and they walked over to Jesse Gibson, who was busy getting their tent ready for the night. They were originally a team of five, and had been put together from their various core groups that had been formed from the beginning. When the core groups had been split up, they'd known it was significant. So they'd decided it was the five of them for the remainder, and had already gotten to know each other deeply during their early days as a team.

Now, though, only four of them remained, and that was one of the reasons this usually cheerful lot seemed somehow quiet, glum. It had been but a few weeks since they were reduced to four, and it had made them all acutely aware of what they were a part of. The seriousness of the situation had sunk in, and although the mood had changed, they were even more determined than before. They all knew they were among the very few who still had any prospects. Something to work for, to stick together for, to do everything possible for.

Maria Solis was the youngest of them at the age of twenty-one. She had been a high school senior when she came to Selection, instead of going to college, like most others her age. Although the Solis family was among the major contributors to the Consortium, she had no guarantees of being on the final list for the mission. Actually she'd expected to be among the first to be cut, but one of the other members of her core group had shown symptoms of mental illness early on, and one day he was simply gone, all his belongings removed and no explanation given. That had given her the necessary time to adjust to the situation. She spent hours upon hours studying, practicing, until finally she seemed to come to grips with some of the areas unfamiliar to her. She'd really struggled with agriculture and biochemistry, which were completely alien to her, but after some initial difficulty, those were areas she came to enjoy. Now she'd turned out to be one of the top students in agriculture and life-support systems, and although she didn't expect to use the latter unless there was a serious emergency en route, she knew she was quietly etching out her little niche that just might earn her a spot.

The others on her team were several years older than she was, with Sophie the closest, both in terms of age and relationship. She was twenty-nine, and already she had made a name for herself in academic circles, being among the top contenders for the prestigious Obama grant when she was picked for Selection. She had once told them how she had been approached by some government types and persuaded to come to Selection, even though she had never shown an interest for anything to do with space. She had reluctantly agreed to come after they had told her they needed knowledgeable people from various backgrounds and professions. Hers was law. Not a likely candidate for space, until now. A once-in-a-lifetime opportunity, they had said. She hadn't really taken any of it seriously in the beginning. How could anyone have known it was the very last opportunity? After this, there would be no more opportunities for anything, for anyone, ever.

The professor, Jeremiah Lowell, wasn't a leader, usually, but in this group, that was the role he had assumed. Maybe it was his age; at forty-seven he was by far the oldest. Turned out the new role suited the professor, and it had stuck, even when others were put to the task. That was not necessarily a good thing, but he had that fatherly charisma that smoothed over most problems, even when he made his opinions clear, loudly, as usual. Maybe it was his concern for others or that strangely twisted way of speaking; who could tell?

The silent one was Jesse Gibson. He sometimes seemed an odd one, and usually took no part in discussions or sides whenever someone argued. But when he did speak up, he was usually right, and his voice and insight always seemed to tip the argument. Introspective, bordering on antisocial, he somehow came to be a natural part of the group, someone they could rely on to complete his tasks in the most efficient manner, whatever they would be, and then help the others out.

The fifth member of the group had been John Rawlins, an engineer with a military background, although he had turned civilian ten years prior to Selection. He was the classic engineer; with bridges, roads, buildings, tunnels, whatever came to mind, he'd done it already. A genuinely nice guy, with one … weakness … one might call it, that eventually caught up with him. Just before leaving for Antarctica, the news of Devastator had finally come out, and Selection took on a new meaning to them all. It was no longer a long series of cuts, training, more cuts, and then, for a lucky few, an adventure that no one really knew anything about, except that it had to do with space. It was about who would live and who would die. Get cut, and you die, simple as that. John was a married man, having left his wife and two kids at their home in Boulder, Colorado to participate in this project. He took the news harder than the rest of them. And one day, he simply packed his belongings, said his good-byes, and went to spend the rest of his time left with his family. Who could blame him?

So here they were, the four of them, setting up camp in the middle of this last wilderness left on Earth. All sounds were muffled, the snow and ice and sheer vastness absorbing most of them, and there was no background noise at all. Will it be something like this in space, Maria wondered. She knew this was nothing compared to space, but still, she felt some familiarizing or something like that had to be their purpose for being here, not just getting used to bulky clothing, face masks, and spending time in a tent. There was usually more to every exercise, every test, and every lecture, than first assumed. Nothing was ever just what it seemed; everything had a specific purpose and an opportunity to grasp some higher meaning, if you only looked beyond the surface of things.

That evening they shared a nice meal together, something Jeremiah had magically cooked up from their usually bland provisions, a mix of canned foods and MREs.

"My secret ingredient," he winked smugly. "I could tell y'all, but then I'd have to kill ya." Maria liked the professor; she really hoped he'd make it through Selection. He did have useful qualifications, but she knew the competition would be harsh until the final names were to be announced. And even then, she wouldn't bet on anything. His age could be a problem. They might be looking for younger people, since some kind of breeding population would obviously be an aspect of this. Then again, he was still here, wasn't he?

"So, what do you guys think?" Maria changed the subject. "What is the destination? Could we colonize the outer solar system somehow?" She didn't direct the question anywhere, but as usual, Jeremiah was the first one to address it. He shook his head.

"Doubt it. Titan or Europa could be habitable, somehow, but they just seem too darn … hostile … I mean, the environments of those two just seem hostile, unfriendly, nothing invitin' about them. They're probably more likely candidates than Mars would have been, had it still existed, and training in Antarctica definitely seems to hit the bull's-eye, but still …"

They all knew the professor sometimes spoke with some of the suits that turned up from time to time, usually whenever there was time for a cut, or some major information to be revealed, although he never shared anything he learned from those brief encounters. But somehow he always seemed to know more than they did, and he was usually a step further along, as information went. So his opinion definitely mattered. Sophie and Jessie had been listening, but weren't really participating in the conjecturing. Sitting quietly, leaning in toward each other, they seemed to have some kind of thing going, although if there was anything more than a tight and mostly quiet friendship, it wasn't obvious to anyone outside their group.

"So what do you really think, Jeremiah?" Maria said. "Are we talking outside the solar system, could it be done? I mean, we'd be talking light years. And the last time I heard we didn't have the means to go any further than Mars. With manned flight that is. And even that was a total screw up." Jesse and Sophie both nodded in agreement. They all knew this story well. It had been decades, but still the memory of how the colonization of Mars had turned into tragedy was part of common knowledge, taught in schools as an example of how NASA, in their final mission, had revealed every negative trait the organization had ever developed. Of course, official history also claimed it showed every negative trait of society as such, and the aftermath of the Mars incident had paved the road for the reforms brought on by Holloway and Andrews. They had never discussed this on the team, but the one thing they all knew was that the Mars incident had meant an effective end to manned space exploration beyond Earth orbit, and when Devastator appeared, it all had to be reassembled from scratch.

"I believe there is a lot to be learned," Jeremiah said. "And it's been what, a little more than four years now, since Mars got blown to pieces. And from the moment someone could see where this was heading, people with considerable resources have been gathering to solve the issues, to create a plan so that we don't go extinct. And I believe the remaining years will be utilized to the fullest; we'll see the absolute pinnacle of human ingenuity. There will be breakthroughs, even up until the last moment, and maybe even beyond launch, so I'd be very wary of saying we can't."

Chapter 7

June 2078 ~ Cambridge, Massachusetts

When Kenneth Taylor, at the age of twenty-six, had washed out of the space academy in Houston, Texas, he thought his life and everything he'd ever dreamed of was over. Before that, he'd been a rising star, with a dual degree in biology and psychology from Harvard, with excellent grades; and his record at the academy up until then had been outstanding. He'd been marked for success, and already stood a good chance at being one of the cadets to be chosen for the Mars mission. Ever since he'd seen John Scott and Oliver Reynolds set their feet upon the surface of the red planet, and with a decent insight for an eleven-year-old kid as to what would be the next great step, his dream had been to one day be among the pioneers to colonize the planet. To be one of the very select few who, as his forefathers had done more than two centuries earlier in the American west, would seek and explore new lands to create a new world.

Throughout the more than two decades that had passed since that dreadful day, which, although it saved his life, did crush his dream of Mars, he'd often wondered how everything could turn out the way it did. He had no good answer to that, and however he phrased the question to himself, whatever angle he chose, he still couldn't understand what really had happened. The facts were simple enough, but the reasons, the reactions, the chain of events—they were still a mystery to him. Now, as a man closing in on fifty years, he sometimes took on an analytical view, to meditate on how the experience had changed him. Of course, there were the apparent changes, like his shift from confident space cadet to renowned academic. With time, his ambitions had recovered and taken on new shapes, and led him to an eventual Harvard professorate, and over the years he'd shown much of the same excellence that had led to such high hopes back when Mars was still the ultimate goal. But the subtle changes, the ones no one really noticed, were perhaps of greater importance as to who he was today. For instance, he never gave away his reactions to people, unless they were part of his agenda, and he'd developed a certain flair for reading people without making it obvious that he did.

Politically, he'd also had quite a development, from being quite ignorant and uninterested to gradually becoming more critical of where the country and the world were headed. He'd started noticing how more and more democratic values and civil rights were being sacrificed in the name of "security." The plague of terrorism that had swept across the world at first bolstered the free world, united them in a common cause. But then, gradually, as time went by and terrorist cells continued to strike, policy shifted toward authoritarianism. When terrorists nuked Seattle, fear seemed to creep into every corner and every critical voice was perceived as a destructive element. America, like most of its allies in the western world, was still a democracy of some sort, but many rights had been revoked, like the right to assembly. These days, if an interest group wanted to legally assemble, they had to be approved by a committee, led by a judge and comprised of two government officials and one layman. The implications were obvious, and this was just one example. Taylor came to resent this development, but public sentiment actually supported it, and he and others of like mind were outnumbered by people who just wanted to live their lives without fear of bombs going off in the streets. He had no problem understanding this, but somehow he felt more and more alienated and isolated from the society in which he had once been such a star.

After Seattle, the critical voices had gone silent, or been subdued by wrecked careers, and sometimes legal action. Some had switched views, due to the horrible acts of terrorism, and chosen what they thought of as the lesser evil. In some cases, the persecution had actually led critics toward more extreme views, and a very few had become involved in terrorist activity. Then there were the likes of Kenneth Taylor. He hadn't been a very vocal critic, which probably was the reason he seemed to escape under the government radar, and after Seattle, he quickly saw the implications. So he went silent. He kept in touch with a few of like mind, but severed his ties to most others. On the surface, there were enough personal and professional reasons to justify him staying in touch with those few that remained, so he never personally experienced any difficulties due to his connections, and it didn't hamper his career any. But when he was alone, the thoughts would come, and he felt like he was the only person in the world who could see the poison that was seeping through the nation. For a long time, he had great difficulty seeing how things could be changed to the better, and although his earlier fall from grace had thickened his skin and made him less prone to despair, he definitely had his black moments.

Kenneth was still unmarried, and when the news of Devastator broke, he was on his yearly hiking trip near Mount Washington with three other bachelor friends. They were taking a break, and when he checked his messages, there was one from one of his research assistants that just said "see news—important!" So he went online, and that's how he learned about the end of the world. Of course, that became the main topic for the rest of the trip, and although it didn't seem real to any of them, he could still remember one of his friends mentioning that for mankind to survive this, they would have to build arks and settle on another planet. Of course, that all seemed like science fiction at the time.

But it was real enough. Three years later, he was called into the office of the head of the Psychology Department, where two government officials greeted him as they got the room to themselves. That's when he learned of the Exodus project and was asked to participate in the selection process out west. When he had asked why he was the one to be approached, as there were almost as many psychologists as there were lawyers, he was told that he wasn't the only one. There were other psychologists out there, but his research had been noticed as groundbreaking where the fields of biology and psychology converged, and his extensive studies on the psychological effects of waking up from a prolonged coma was also an asset that separated him from most. By then, selection had been going on for four years, but he was told that his entry would not be unusual; at times, new candidates would enter, as the plans developed, and needs arose, and he was one of those late candidates. Actually, the first launches were less than a year away, so he had to leave immediately. At that moment, he rediscovered hope. There would be a new world out there, like a tabula rasa, a blank page, waiting for whatever would fill it. That was the moment he made a silent vow to himself that his role would not be limited to what the government officials intended. It was too early to fully comprehend the implications, or to consciously figure out how to make an actual impact. He just knew that this was a chance to make a better world than the one he'd leave behind, and he'd be damned if he didn't grab that chance with both hands and hold tight. As he shook hands with them, he knew that the opportunity he could only have dreamed of had arrived. As much as the prospect of Earth dying was a miserable one, he couldn't help it. He felt excited, beyond anything he'd ever felt in his entire life.

"Today, we're going to have a discussion. I expect everyone to contribute to this. You will be graded, and as you all know, final selection is only a few months away, and your grades will count." Maria met Sophie's eyes for an instant; they both knew they were far from safe. Sophie's relationship with Jesse had almost made her quit after Jesse had been cut, and although she'd dived deep into her studies and projects, everyone knew she'd had a period of doubts and low motivation. Of course, the instructors had also noticed that, and it didn't sit well with them. Maria had continued to do well in her main chosen areas of agriculture and life support, but she'd had a difficult time trying to support her friend, and while that would be seen as an asset by instructors, they also saw that she'd come to depend too much on another, which would be counterproductive to her own development. So many considerations ... And really, who knew what would eventually count, come final selection?

Dr. Tanaka paced slowly in front of them, chewing his old-fashioned pencil, as he usually did, while choosing his words.

"I expect you to have speculated on where your destination will be. Many of you will have read extensively on planetary habitability, solar analogs, and so forth. I can tell you right now that when the time came, some two years ago, when a choice had to be made, it was not an easy one. In the years prior to our discovery of Devastator, several exoplanets had already been found, using different techniques, such as Earth-based telescopes, Doppler detection, and telescopes able to observe star occultation. However, the number of possible habitable planets was low, so after Devastator came into the equation, the studies began to focus on a small number of systems.

"The basic criteria to be a candidate were that the planet would have to be in the habitable zone around a star analogue to our own sun. The habitable zone, to those of you who haven't read up on this, is the zone where an Earth-like planet can maintain liquid water and possibly harbor life. To pick a star similar to our own is really a practical consideration; we still don't know exactly what it would take to support life around, say, a red dwarf, for a long period of time, so we made it a little simpler for ourselves. Red dwarves could support life, but they are noted to sometimes flare up, which would kill everything alive. This can probably be predicted, but why bother? There are better options. There was also the question of mass. Stars smaller than the sun have habitable zones with planets that might be conducive to life.

However, the habitable zones of such stars would be a whole lot closer to the star, making such planets prone to larger tides. This might remove the axial tilt, which would make seasons disappear. One downside to that is that the poles would be colder and the equator would be damn hot. Also, that close to the star, the day and year could be synchronized, meaning one side of the planet would always face the star, while the other remained in permanent night. This would give us a number of problems, like one side being way too hot and the other frozen, although on average it would look nice. Since there is no way to know the details before you arrive, we couldn't take a chance on that.

"Of course, distance has been an important variable, but our solutions to the distances involved in each scenario are still experimental. Variable stars were excluded, and we decided to focus on stars that showed signs of being rich in metals, since that would give us nice rocky planets, rich in necessary resources and tectonic activity. We didn't want to spend time on gas giants, which could possibly harbor habitable moons, since we don't know enough about them. What we wanted was a habitable solid planet, a nice ball of solid rock, like Earth. And since we had found a few of those, we chose to focus on them. We then studied what data we had, and found five candidates that could be proven to have the elements needed to sustain life as we know it, that is carbon, hydrogen, oxygen, and nitrogen. As some of you will note, we would definitely need phosphorus and sulfur as well, but we're unable to detect that from Earth.

"We then focused on orbits, that is, we need a fairly circular orbit to avoid extreme variations in temperature. We could to some degree adapt to that, but it would be a difficulty best avoided. That ruled out another two. There were several other considerations that I won't bother you with, but in the end a decision was made."

Maria almost held her breath. If she hadn't been so intent on what was to come, she would have noticed everyone shifting a little, backs straightening, eyes wide open, as Dr. Tanaka stopped moving and signaled one of his assistants to dim the lights a bit so that his presentation would show better.

"Approximately 40.3 light years away, we find 55 Cancri, a binary system located in the constellation of Cancer. The system consists of a yellow dwarf, like our sun, and a smaller red dwarf, separated by over 1,000 Astronomical Units, that is; one thousand times the distance from Earth to the sun. The primary, 55 Cancri A, has an apparent magnitude of 5.95, and is just barely visible to the naked eye under very dark skies. The red dwarf 55 Cancri B is only visible through a telescope. We shall focus on the primary here, since, as many of you by now have guessed, this is where we find our chosen planet."

"Excuse me, sir," a skinny redheaded woman Maria had only seen a couple times before interrupted. "I don't mean to interrupt, but …" Dr. Tanaka turned toward her and motioned for her to rise.

"Ah excellent, finally someone who dares to take part. Don't be shy, young lady, please speak up. Oh, and please state your name for us, I believe you haven't all been introduced to each other."

"Okay, ah … Well … my name is Karin Svensson, please excuse my English …" She stuttered a bit, clearly nervous, with every eye upon her. She fumbled with her notes, then decided to put them back down on her chair.

"Where are you from, Ms. Svensson?" That was Dr. Tanaka again. He could be a hard nail in class, but he also liked a good discussion. Though he could lose himself in monologue from time to time, he had a curiosity that allowed him to appreciate differing views, a trait that probably made him a very good teacher.

"I'm from Sweden, sir. I was with ESA before I came here." This could be interesting, Maria thought. The European Space Agency had contributed greatly to the planet-finding efforts, and after NASA was disbanded, space studies in general fell from grace in the U.S. Ever since, ESA had been the world's leading community for astronomy and astrobiology.

"Well, what I was wondering was what your thoughts would be on our final candidate being a binary? Binaries are not thought to be very conducive to habitable planets, since the gravity of two stars could affect the orbits of planets. Have you found actual evidence that this is not the case here?"

Dr. Tanaka smiled, and nodded to himself.

"You're right of course; that was common knowledge among astronomers for a long time. At first, because it is common sense; with two stars pulling at a planet from different angles, one should expect the planetary orbit to take on really odd shapes. This would present serious obstacles, to say the least, because there would be extreme variations in surface temperature. For a long time this was the general consensus within the scientific community. It wasn't until a 2009 paper on the properties of Alpha Centauri, that this was disputed. The study showed that Centauri A and B, having a distance of at least eleven AU, had stable habitable zones. This of course meant that planets within those zones could perhaps support life. Actually, the results showed that planets within a distance of three AU of either star could have stable orbits. I guess I've lost some of you already, but this is important, as it shows how little we know, and how much of a gamble this project really is. Okay, as you, Ms. Svensson, probably know, this study was the groundwork on further studies by NASA, ESA, SETI, and others concerning the possible habitability of Alpha Centauri, and although the results were dubious, the conclusion was that the 2009 study must have erred somehow, as the planets that were finally discovered had orbits that ruled out any possibility of habitability, at least for life as we know it. And that was basically the end of binaries as possible new worlds for future human exploration, and search for life continued elsewhere. Then, just before Devastator was discovered, new findings indicated that the 2009 study had actually been onto something, only that the distances they claimed were wrong. The distance between stars had to be at least 180 AUs, which of course excluded Alpha Centauri. But for systems where the stars are further apart, the gravitational effects will be negligible on planets orbiting an otherwise suitable star. These new findings were never published, as the discovery of

Devastator got all the attention of the scientists. But a small number of people worked on this and everything we've found so far supports the thesis." He paused, took a small sip of water, and smiled broadly.

"I've already told you, we found the orbits of planets around 55 Cancri to be stable, simply put. And what's more, we found every basic element that is needed to support life on one of the planets. Not just the elements, but the general geological features as well. It has an atmosphere, possibly not very different from our own, although it is impossible to be certain at this time. We expect there to be differences, but it is really impossible to know the exact composition from this distance. It seems promising though, and definitely good enough to protect colonists from radiation and so forth. The destination planet is the fifth out from the primary, and it has been given the name Aurora. And as science moves forward, so does the equipment. Just recently we've been able to conduct a spectral analysis of the light emitted from Aurora itself, and the findings were, to say the least, interesting … We found evidence of photosynthesis. You all know what that means. Ladies and gentlemen, we found life."

Maria was stunned. She hadn't expected this, and nearly skipped a heartbeat as Dr. Tanaka let the truth of that sentence sink in. Life. Finally, as life on Earth came to its close, the greatest question of all time had been answered. We are not alone! she thought.

"Of course, we are unable to know whether life means intelligent life or plants or microbial life. We don't have the means to study that, and only those of you who survive final selection will ever be able to find out. But life means both new opportunities and new dangers. It could mean more easily obtainable food, or it could mean spores or bacteria that could kill you. Or, less likely but still possible, intelligent life. That would raise more questions; will it be benign or hostile? How could we prepare for either, what could be done in advance to increase the likelihood of such an encounter being a success and not a final and devastating blow to the last remnants of humanity? Life. This changes everything. And that's what I want you to work on for tomorrow. That's right, I'm giving you an assignment. We'll continue discussing our designated target, but right now I want you to write down your assignment, then take a short break. We'll start again in ten minutes. I'll expect you to be a lot more engaged when we resume: ask questions, voice opinions, look at things from different angles, like Ms. Svensson just did. Remember, you're being graded for participation. I guess that should be even more of a motivator now."

The first launches were only weeks away, and there was a much more competitive mood in the compound these days. The candidates that remained knew that not all of them would be on the final list, and that sometimes brought out the worst in them. Cheating seemed commonplace, and there had been several instances of even close friends sabotaging each other's projects and assignments. If someone seemed to get too much praise, or do too well on tests, they were disdained by the others. And of course, everybody hated the newcomers.

Kenneth Taylor understood that all too well. It wasn't just the competitiveness; it was also a basic instinct for survival. Devastator was coming, and the latest predictions said it would hit Earth in a little more than five years. There was a margin of error, but the closer it got, the more certain the predictions were. A direct hit. The worst possible outcome. By now, there were so few candidates left that everybody felt they stood a decent chance. Humans are funny that way, Taylor thought. In the face of certain death, men will show great courage, make great sacrifices, show a selfless determination to complete an impossible task. But if there is a slight chance they might actually get out of a sticky situation by sacrificing their friends or their ideals, the dark side of mankind shows itself. Taylor had long since concluded that humans could be both selfless and selfish; it all came down to the situation. So, in this particular situation, most candidates acted according to their nature, sad as it was. But he understood. If the astronomers were right, everybody knew what would happen to those who didn't make the cut. The greatest adventure in human history seemed a far more tempting prospect than the greatest disaster.

"I heard Carol Larkin had to go last night." That was Geena Travis, the girl he'd been teamed up with when he arrived just two weeks ago. There were three others on the team, but he couldn't see them anywhere. He guessed they were back at H Building, studying, or maybe plotting how to get ahead on tomorrow's advanced technical aptitude test. He had always thought that the human machinery works best on a full stomach, so here he was in the big dining hall, enjoying a nice after-dinner Italian coffee and Tiramisu with Geena, whom he'd quickly learned to like.

Geena Travis was a twenty-three-year-old girl, still in high school when she was picked for Selection five years ago. A pretty blonde, always with a smile on her face, and a positive outlook on life, she sometimes provoked people who didn't share her attitudes. She had often been underestimated, based on that big smile, long blonde hair, and typical high school cheerleader appearance. Kenneth Taylor wouldn't dream of making such a mistake. As a college professor, he'd often seen the most unlikely freshmen excel when put in an environment that reinforced their innate abilities. He'd seen assumingly mindless cheerleaders and high school losers go on to PhDs and astonishing careers in business, academia, or government. As he'd gotten to know her better, he'd discovered a keen mind and a talent for coming up with creative answers to questions that most candidates had to struggle hard to figure out. In addition to an athletic body that would stand more rigors than he'd only dreamed of coping with, and a psychological makeup that would make her less prone to depression in the face of adversity or even disaster, she was surely a top candidate.

"That right?" Taylor answered.

"I really thought she was going to make it. She seemed the type." They both hunched their shoulders, taking another sip of coffee, and Taylor discovered he'd eaten most of his cake too. Typical me, he thought. I always get too distracted to really enjoy the pleasures of life, like this cake.

"Yeah," Geena continued. "You never really know what they are looking for. Or what their selection criteria are. Who knows, we might be next." Her cheerful disposition didn't allow for her to dwell on things like that, and it only took about ten seconds before she changed the subject.

"You know, I don't think Devastator means the end of the world. I think it just means some sort of cleansing, a new chance. Nothing like the cultists say," she hastily added. "I am a Christian, you know, sort of anyway, but that kind of BS doesn't have anything to do with Christianity, if you ask me. God's punishment and all that." She shook her head and peered into her empty cup. When she spoke again, it was a little strained.

"No, I think it will be a nightmare. And that a lot of people, most I guess, will die. But some will survive. I have to believe that. We all have to believe that. And from there, anything could happen." Taylor smiled sadly at her. He very much wanted to believe the same. He knew that she knew of the latest predictions. He just didn't have as much faith as she did. She was determined to keep her belief that some good had to come out of this, even here on Earth. His hopes, on the other hand, lay in the possibility of a better world on Aurora.

They rose and walked back to H Building to meet their team. They had individual tests tomorrow, so there was no need to work together. Just as well, Taylor thought. The others seemed much too concerned with the competition than with the actual tasks at hand. As they entered the apartment they shared, they saw that only Hans Kleve, the Danish shuttle pilot, remained. There were no sign of the others, or their belongings.

"Where are ..." Geena was interrupted by Hans, who waved her off.

"The instructors came just fifteen minutes ago and took them away. They didn't give an explanation." He sat slumped on the couch. He'd just lost two of his best buddies and seemed to believe he was next in line. He'd never excelled at anything, but his team had been a good one for a long time now. Taylor suspected that it was mostly due to Geena and didn't mourn the loss. Of course, that was something he didn't state out loud.

"I'm sorry, Hans. I know how much they meant to you." Hans just stared emptily at the open door, as if waiting for the instructors to come barging in to carry him off. Away from his one chance to live. Taylor knew in his heart that it was actually the most likely outcome for him.

Chapter 8

When they decided on a name for the starship, they had considered several alternatives. In the end, it only seemed fitting to keep the name of the project itself. Everything they had worked toward, their entire focus was the creation of their means for escape… and survival: the starship. So, even though it still only existed in parts and modules orbiting the Earth, the ship was named the Exodus. Captain Tina Hammer thought it was a good name, because it carried the entire story of the massive endeavor: from despair, to escape, and finally hope. As she checked the few personal belongings she had packed, one last time, she could hear the rumble of artillery in the distance. Sometimes she could feel the shaking from an impact nearby. There were thousands of armed attackers surrounding the launch site, and some Army and Air Force contingents had even joined with the rebels. Those of the Air Force had been swiftly dealt with, and although they had been able to shoot down two of the launches, there were no enemy planes in the air any more. However, the loyal troops had taken quite a beating, and the frontlines had gradually crept closer to the compound during the last week. Its fall seemed inevitable; it was just a question of time now. Tina had serious doubts about whether they would be able to hold off the insurgents long enough for the last few launches to be completed.

This morning, the fighting seemed particularly fierce, and she hurried over to the bus that would take her to the pre-launch facility, where she would be prepped for launch, together with the others who were to be sent up into orbit today. There would be about thirty this time, in a shuttle crammed to the limit, as the final launches had been expedited to account for the fact that they were losing ground to the rebels. Tina knew there were three more launches scheduled, but hers was the last manned shuttle. They were only able to launch one mission a day, and although at times there had been as many as three or four launches a day, it was still a staggering efficiency, compared to earlier practices. Of course, that also entailed a higher risk, as the ground crews were all exhausted, working around the clock to keep this schedule. She could only admire them; they had no ticket out of here, and their prospects when the compound was overrun were bleak.

The bus took them out from the housing facilities and on a thirty-minute ride to pre-launch. The route took them a little too close to the frontlines for her to feel comfortable. She'd seen combat before, but this was different. This was America, and on both sides were desperate Americans firing

November 2079 ~ Somewhere in Arizona

at each other. She shook her head at the idea, which just a few months ago had seemed impossible.

The air was filled with smoke, and visibility was only a few meters. Coming around a bend, suddenly the bus was forced to stop, held at gunpoint by armed men wearing gas masks. They were uniformed, and although that didn't count for much these days, they seemed disciplined enough. The passengers were briskly commanded to exit the vehicle, and inspected in a thorough but expedient manner.

"All right," said a masked man with chevrons on his sleeves. "You can continue, but you'd better hurry up. The lines are breaching in this area, and this road will be overrun in a few hours. There have been several attempts at infiltration, and yesterday a bus rigged with a bomb went off just before it reached pre-launch."

"Why would anybody do that, Sergeant?" Tina said as she passed him walking back to her seat. "They seem desperate, of course, but blowing up the launch facilities would only ensure that no one gets out." She was puzzled by the news, and the sergeant nodded.

"That's right, ma'am, but the rebels are a mix of all kinds. Most of them wouldn't dream of harming the facility, although we are fair game. But there are some, especially the extreme religious folks, that believe the launches should be stopped because of God's will or something. They seem to believe that all this is God's righteous punishment or something. And that we should just accept it and pray for a miracle." The sergeant shook his head. "Damn fools …"

"Well, praying for miracles wouldn't hurt I guess, but let's keep it at that." Tina managed a strained smile before reentering the bus. She had a deep respect for those men and women who would most likely never make it through the day, but still performed their duties, to make sure that Project Exodus made it into the next phase.

The next phase, of course, would consist of all modules of the Exodus assembled in orbit, a process that was estimated to take approximately six months to complete. Only then would the crew and passengers board the ship that would be their home for 165 years until they reached Aurora. The launch schedule had been set up so that all critical parts had already been put into orbit. They had always suspected this kind of situation, hence the heavy military presence and a launch schedule that allowed for losses, without it seriously damaging the mission.

Tina suspected that hers might turn out to be the last launch, and she wasn't even sure there would be enough time for that. She could only hope the lines would hold long enough, but they had cut the time prior to launch to the bone, there was simply no way to make it any faster. They needed two hours in the pre-launch facility, then they would board the shuttle, which took about an hour, and then finally there would be a fifteen-minute countdown before launch. Her experience and instincts told her that there would be no tomorrow for the soldiers she'd just talked to, and that the launch facilities wouldn't survive the takeover by rebels. Too many heavily armed and trigger-happy people with nothing to lose, drugs and alcohol in abundance, and probably no established chain of command. The damage and killings would be unchecked, there would be no purpose left for them but rampant destruction.

They arrived twenty minutes late, and she was hurried along into pre-launch. There she went through her final medical checkup, and was quickly outfitted and readied for launch. She saw one of her buddies from Selection when she entered the bridge that took her the last stretch over to the shuttle. It was Lieutenant Henry Carroll, and they nodded to each other. She didn't know who else would be on the same shuttle, as they had been separated for almost a year, but she knew that Kim Leffard and Dean Johnson had been on one of the first launches and were already in orbit. Entering the shuttle, she recognized another two faces; Lowell, the geology professor, and a young girl with Latino features whose name she didn't remember. They were all strapped in, and then all they could do was wait for countdown to commence.

The launch was successful and there were no problems during their flight to orbit. A few hours later, they lost radio contact with the launch pad, but based on the last messages received, they all knew the compound had been overrun. Tina thought about the last frenzied effort of the workers down there that had made her launch possible. As a veteran of more than one conflict, she'd often been called a hero, but the way she saw it, the real heroes were those workers. She could only hope they would be spared, but she didn't expect it.

A week went by, and Tina had just started reading a big chunk of documents she needed to go through before they were to board the Exodus. As the executive officer of the starship, she had to be ready at all times to assume command, as she was the replacement for the commander himself whenever he was away from the bridge or had to delegate responsibilities. They were still stuck in the shuttle though; it would be some time before they could enter the starship itself, it was still being assembled by hundreds of workers and quite a few bots at the moment, so she had plenty of reading time on her hands. They were just settling into their routines as a surprising call came through the comms system. It was a kid's voice.

"This is the New Discovery, final launch from ... uhm ... anyways, we're on autopilot or something, and we need to ... ah, slave to you, I think it's called." What the kid was describing was an automated procedure that allowed two shuttles to dock, where one would slave its systems and be controlled by the other, in order to synchronize their approach. The shuttle pilot, Lieutenant Frank Pollock, answered, and though he looked every bit as puzzled as the rest of them, his voice was as steady as ever.

"This is Lieutenant Pollock of the San Francisco, we read you loud and clear. Please identify yourself, son." There was a moment of silence before the kid answered.

"Ah, this is Ben, ah, Benjamin Waters, sir. What do you need me to do?"

"I'll need your docking codes. You'll find them on the left of the main screen, four words and an eight-digit number. I need to punch those manually into the computer here. Then we'll take over and do the rest."

Later, as the shuttles were connected, and the hatch of the New Discovery opened, Tina and the others were both curious and anxious as to what would happen. She feared there might be armed men on board, but the fact that it had been a kid manning the shuttle suggested that there would be no adults there at all. And when the kids flowed through the hatch, she could clearly see that they were all just children, from the age of six and up through sixteen or seventeen. There were thirty-five kids on the shuttle, and while they exceeded the shuttle's limit as to numbers, their ages made several of them so light that the total weight limit had held.

Benjamin Waters was the oldest at seventeen; he had naturally taken charge. He seemed like the natural leader, although his age made him insecure when meeting those on the San Francisco, being captains, lieutenants, professors, and so on. He told them the amazing tale of how they had ended up on the shuttle.

"Some of these kids are children of rebel leaders, while others are here mostly by chance. I was rounded up by the rebels two months ago, and conscripted, sort of, to lead a squad of younger kids. We were supposed to carry ammunitions for the artillery, and although we were lucky, not just cannon fodder at the front, we lost one kid, a fifteen-year-old girl called Wendy, to an air raid three weeks ago. It was bad, really bad …" Tina could see the boy struggled when he recalled the memories, but Ben, as he was called, managed to keep his emotions in check.

"Well, anyways, when I arrived at the compound, it had been a few hours since we took it. A lot of people died that day … But one of the leaders, General Hayden, had ordered the launch facility and staff to be spared, and put a death penalty, like shoot on sight, on those who dared disobey that order. He was serious about it too, and even shot two men himself for trying to rape a female technician." He shuddered and closed his eyes for a second before he continued.

"That order saved a lot of lives though, and the facility stayed mostly unscathed. Of course, in the heat of battle, there had been some damages, so we were only able to get one of the remaining shuttles launch capable.

"The general said our mission was to save some of the future, and that getting a small number of children away was the only reason he had for breaking his allegiances. He said it was the reason he had joined forces with the rebels in the first place. He picked kids, mostly at random, although his daughter Lisa is on board too, to be sent, and I have no idea how I could be even considered for this. I've never done anything technical, and up until the rebels overran my hometown, I was just a high school kid. I never wanted to be in charge of anything, but the general put me in charge. I don't know why, I never wanted ..." Tina saw Ben shake and shut his eyes, losing the battle against the memories walled in by necessity. She'd seen it so many times, in hardened soldiers and people forced into situations that demanded a cool that was unnatural for them.

"I just want you to know that we never wanted all this, all the killing ... Anyways, it took a week to get ready for launch, and by that time, things had calmed down. It seemed there was some kind of truce, so there were no air raids on the facility either. I guess the Air Force had been told about the general's intention to put kids into the shuttle, and they probably thought it was a good idea too. I don't think anybody fully understood how the smaller kids would react though. Since we've been strapped in the shuttle, me and some of the other older kids have been busy trying to calm the younger kids. Some went hysterical right away; others went sick and puked all the way up. Right now, I think most of them are just too exhausted to scream or anything. Frankly, I'm afraid some of them are permanently damaged by all this. But I guess when it's all about survival, then … Well, I mean … The adults probably knew it would be hard on the kids. But it's better than staying down there, right?

"Anyways, I know there weren't supposed to be any more manned launches, so I guess us being here is a problem …" Tina interrupted him and placed a hand on his shoulder.

"It's okay, Ben. You can relax now. We do have a challenge, with more passengers and less supplies, but we'll deal with that. You're coming to Aurora with us, and we're all in this together now." Then she smiled at him.

"You seem like a good kid, and I for one welcome you on board. I think you've done great, and you shouldn't be blamed for other people's actions. You shouldn't blame yourself either. That's important." The others nodded in agreement. The additional passengers did pose a serious difficulty, but they would handle it somehow. Right now they were all safe, at least for the time being.

January 2080 ~ Earth orbit

Greg Hamilton, admiral and commander of the Exodus, was a graying man of fifty-two years, who had never had any family since he left his foster home at the age of sixteen to join the Navy. Even so, he had come to understand the importance of family and why family made people make decisions that weren't always fully rational. Right now, he had the consequences of one such decision to deal with. At the moment, orbiting Earth while final preparations were being made, his problem was that there were more people on board than they had planned for.

"Okay then, give me the numbers again," he said while going through the latest calculations on his tablet. The executive officer, Major Tina Hammer, had her own tablet, and once more recited the numbers. Total fuel resources, acceleration fuel consumption, estimated oxygen reproduction rate, and so on.

"All in all, sir, the fuel is sufficient. Even if we spend all the fuel in the acceleration phase, the reactors will produce more than enough for the energy consumption during transit and deceleration. There will even be a buffer left in the case of unforeseen incidents."

"All right, Tina, that's reassuring. And life support seems good too. So, it seems the main problem still is the cryostasis issue."

"Yes, sir. Currently there are 1,628 people on board, while there are only 1,610 cryo cells, including the ones we put in for redundancy. At 25 percent of light speed on average, and given the conservative deceleration option, we have a total travel time of approximately 165 years. The time dilation effect will cut about four years off, but we'll adjust to Earth time for practical purposes, as relativity can be confusing, which is something we don't need. Anyway, the math on the passenger problem is actually quite simple. The only viable solution seems to be to manually override the cryo cell controls to have a part of the crew awake at all times. That way, the crew may age a couple of years each, but we'll be able to bring everyone to Aurora with the resources at hand. The added food and oxygen consumption will be averted by tighter rationing and a shorter time in orbit once we arrive. It will be tight, but we'll make it." The commander nodded. He knew that was what they would have to do, if they were to bring everyone along. The only problem was the risk involved with an untested technology. Cryo tech was a completely new invention, derived from medical experimentation and developed during the hectic years of the project.

"They never tested how multiple periods of cryo sleep would affect humans, you know. There are theories about that though. And we do have the escape pods ..."

"Sir, if I may ..." Hammer obviously couldn't help but insist, and Hamilton let her speak. He, for one, appreciated officers who spoke frankly, and Hammer was that kind. She would voice her opinions as long and as loudly as it took, and when the decision was made, she'd stand by it and support her senior officer. It was the kind of loyalty shown by officers with potential for senior command.

"I wouldn't feel comfortable sending the kids back down. And who would you choose to go instead? It would be a death sentence, most likely. Yes, I know we have the escape pods, but we might need them at arrival. And, sir, this whole thing is experimental. One more unknown is something we can live with." Hamilton squinted; he had to think about the interests of the crew and passengers as a whole. What if this one detail was the thing that jeopardized the chances of the survival of mankind?

"I need something better, Tina. You know what's at stake here." Hammer seemed to have put a great deal of thought into this, because she actually did produce a solution.

"It's rather simple, sir. Uncomfortable, but simple. You make sure there are qualified persons awake on first watch. They test the ones waking up after two years in cryo. Then, two years later, those people are put to sleep again, and you wake them again two years later, to repeat the process, searching for cell damages, different readings on vitals and so forth. If any of the tests are positive, you have two years for follow up studies. After eight years you'll have enough data to know whether it's safe to continue rotation. If it is, fine, then we'll have one less thing to worry about. If it's not safe, you have the same choice as you have now; who will live and who will die. The difference is that if we do this, we'll know. The choice will be a necessary one, and you can prove why it is necessary." Hammer paused, then added, "Of course, the authority lies with you, and I'm sure the crew will back any decision you make. But if the choice were mine, I'd make sure it was a decision that absolutely cannot be questioned. I would hate to know that I sent people to their deaths unnecessarily." Hamilton looked at her and knew she wanted to add something, but he motioned for her to keep quiet. What Hammer had just touched upon was a minefield, and she knew it. As the commander of military men and women, he would never have problems whether the decision went one way or the other, he trusted his people to follow his lead. With the civilians, on the other hand, it was less predictable. Havelar and the president had assured him that everyone on board had been through a thorough screening, and there should be no doubts concerning loyalty; but they were referring to political loyalty. There were many forms of loyalty, and there was no way to know how things would play out on Aurora. Old loyalties might change. He was normally not one to let political concerns or questions of how he would be perceived influence his decisions, but Hammer did have a point. And besides, Hamilton had his own qualms about sending anyone on what was basically a life raft back into the water.

"I see your point. And I think it might be worth a shot. We both want to save as many as we can." He clasped his hands behind his back, and turned. "Gather the medical scientists and biologists to get their views on how to actually do this, and get life support in on it too. Having people awake during the journey will eat into our supplies, but your estimates make sense. If we ration the food and adjust the life-support systems, there shouldn't be much of a problem. And of course, you'll need the cryo technicians to adjust the couches to enable switching between people. I'm putting you in charge of this, Tina. I want you to be awake when we wake those people second time around. I count on you to do what's necessary if things don't turn out the way we're hoping for." He saw the determination in the eyes of the young woman; they both knew what that meant. And they both knew that, if necessary, Hammer would make sure it was done swiftly and painlessly.

Chapter 9

February 2080 ~ Somewhere in Arizona

The message on Senator Joe Buchanan's tablet was encrypted with an algorithm that took several seconds to decipher, and he waited impatiently for the words to appear. He knew it had to be important, or else Thatcher would never have contacted him in person. After the initial meeting where Joe was introduced to the conspiracy, they had only spoken once in person, and only a few times by phone. These days, as the Exodus was so close to departure, even encrypted messages were few. Finally the message became legible, and Joe started. The FBI was onto them. A brave young man of the lower ranking cadres of the group had been arrested months ago, but that had been a ploy to divert the hounds from the real objective of what they were doing. Now the feds were getting too close for comfort. In the message, Thatcher wrote that the FBI had finally been able to figure out the purpose and partially the extent of the conspiracy. He also wrote that he expected the FBI to arrest him within the next twenty-four hours, and he advised Joe to go underground immediately. The message ended with a simple good-bye, and Joe sat back in his high-backed office chair, breathing heavily. It was time to make his exit; that much was obvious. He felt sad for his friend, who had been such an idealist and an inspiration to everyone involved. As head of Project Exodus, he'd gradually met other members of the group, and a few uninitiated with similar views on what kind of society the new world should be. While few mentioned Thatcher's name, several gave the impression that they'd been talking to this man who had opened their eyes to what the possibility for a second chance on Aurora really meant. Now he knew in his heart that he'd never see him again; if Thatcher knew the feds were coming, they couldn't be far off.

He finally stood up, and walked across the room. On the wall, he had a framed picture of him and his wife, Cecilia. It had been taken on their honeymoon to Greece; it had to be at least three decades ago now. He beheld it fondly for a moment. They had been so young, so in love. They still were. He smiled at the thought; he'd had a good marriage and a wife that gave him comfort and filled his life with warmth and meaning. They had accepted the fact that they could never have children, and although it made them both sad at times, it had made them embrace what they had even more. When they first met, he'd told her he'd never met anyone who could even measure up to her; it was still the simple truth. Now, he only saw her on the weekends, as she had been reluctant to come out west with him. He always felt bad when he couldn't be with her every day, but after many years in public service, they both knew the demands of the job. It was Thursday, and he sometimes managed to get home on Thursday evenings. He had a flight scheduled for tonight, and he'd been looking forward to a quiet evening at home. He sighed heavily, and lifted the picture from the wall before he turned it around. On the back there was a taped piece of paper, with a twelve-digit number. It was old fashioned, he knew, but at least the possibility of electronic interception was eliminated. Then he typed the number into a special application on his tablet, and got a new number, which he dialed on his phone. The number enabled the encryption of conversations on the phone. Although not as secure as the encryption used for his messages on the tablet, it would do for now. If anyone with the right equipment tried to break it, it would still take them a couple of hours, which was all the time he needed. He waited for a few seconds, until Deacon Frost answered. He'd been an Air Force lieutenant when they first met, and when Buchanan was appointed director of Project Exodus, he'd made sure that Frost had gradually been able to advance to the Selection Board, which made the real decisions on who would be going on the starship. Joe had once mentioned that maybe they should get Deacon a seat on the Exodus, to carry on his work there. The younger man had declined. He said that his place was back on Earth, that he could do more there, even though they both knew the likelihood of survival after impact.

"Deacon," he said. The voice on the other end wouldn't have expected him to call directly, as they tried not to have more contact than would be perceived naturally.

"It's time." Frost said nothing, but he could hear his breathing change subtly.

"What about you wife, sir?" The younger man replied quickly. Buchanan had given that a lot of thought lately. He'd never let his wife know what he was up to, basically to protect her. But he knew that if the FBI got her, they would assume she knew something, and the interrogation would be rough. He chose to put that thought away; he had to steel himself. And who could tell, if all went well they would be able to reunite later.

"I'll make sure she gets away, but I can't take her with me." The risk is too great, he thought. He would gladly have taken on the risk himself, but there were others who depended on him too.

"All right, sir. I'll have the car ready in fifteen minutes."

"Good." He put down the phone and went to hang the picture back in its place on the wall. Then he sat down for a moment before he dialed his wife's number. When she answered, his eyes almost watered, and his throat constricted for a second, before he was able to talk.

"Cecilia," he said. There was no way back. "It's me, dear. I won't be able to come home tonight."

February 2080 ~ Columbus, Ohio

When Special Agent Robert Marsden received his orders, he was getting ready to go camping with his wife and three kids. They had been planning this trip for some time now, and the weather forecast had been good. It had been almost a year since the last one, and the kids had been talking about this for weeks. The cabin had been reserved, and the car was already packed, when Special Agent Tom Wilkie called.

"What's up, Tom?" Robert asked. Tom wouldn't call him outside of work unless something was wrong.

"Well, first off, all leaves and vacations are being put off." Damn, Robert thought, so much for camping.

"You are to report back to the office within an hour. Seems we have a crisis on our hands. I'll fill you in with the details once you get here, but this is big." He didn't have to say anything else. Marsden had been on the job long enough to know that when agents were recalled like this, it had to be big. His wife, fully understanding the nature of his work, never made a fuss about it, and the kids were old enough to understand too. So he quickly changed clothes, checked his gun and badge, and got into his car.

Robert had never seen the director in person before. A few years ago, the old director had paid them a half an hour visit, as a publicity stunt, visiting half a dozen local branches in one day, but other than that, they seldom saw anyone above branch around here. Now, while the agents were gathering in the briefing room, the director paced impatiently back and forth. FBI Director Anthony Barron was a heavyset black man somewhere in his fifties, with a fat mustache, a commanding voice, and eyes that seemed to take in every detail around him.

"I'll make this short," he said to the agents as the shuffling and whispers subsided. "Six months ago, we found evidence of a conspiracy involving senior officials in this administration. We knew something was going on that had to do with Project Exodus, but we had no idea of who was involved or what the conspiracy was all about. The only person we actually apprehended was an executive at the Energy Department, and he didn't really give us anything. Because of his work, which involved insight and connections within the nuclear energy sector, we quickly suspected sabotage, which so far has turned out to be impossible to prove. The Exodus is now fully assembled, and is scheduled to leave Earth orbit within the week. We cannot rule out that there may be a suicide bomber on board, but so far, we have found nothing to indicate that. For a while we suspected a link between this particular conspiracy and the insurrection out west, but this doesn't fit the profile. The insurrection didn't seem to have any real political goals, as far as we can tell. It was likely just the result of desperate human beings who resorted to illogical actions. The only thing they actually achieved was to send a bunch of kids into space, and otherwise wreak havoc in the final stages of launch. If their goals had anything to do with hampering the progress of the project, they failed miserably. And after the kids managed to reach orbit, the leaders actually gave themselves up, one after the other. Did you know that General Hayden actually surrendered an entire army division before committing suicide? Nah, like I said, this has nothing to do with the insurrection. In the last few days however, we have found evidence that the conspiracy at hand involves a plan to select certain individuals for the Exodus that have grudges against the government, or at least the current administration. We don't know the extent of this, so we cannot tell how many there are, if any. We certainly don't have the names of these individuals yet. However, just this morning, we arrested Richard Thatcher, one of the senior executives at PAEI. With the proper drugs and treatment by our interrogation specialists, he soon spilled his guts." There were a few low chuckles around. They all knew what "interrogation specialists" meant.

"He was unable to give us much detail though, having already injected an irreversible lethal poison before his apprehension. But we did get a name."

Robert and Tom approached the front entrance carefully, with other agents covering every door and window on all sides of the large white house. It was past midnight and the garden was lit with light posts. The house itself was completely dark, except a single light at the front door. This was the house of Senator Joe Buchanan, and according to their research he should have taken his usual flight back home earlier this evening. By now, he was probably sound asleep. They had a warrant for his arrest for conspiracy and treason. Their orders were to make all efforts to take him alive, so they were armed mostly with non-lethal weapons, although they had their firearms just in case there were others on the premises. Tom banged at the door.

"Federal agents! Come out with your hands on your head!" he shouted loudly. No response. They waited for maybe half a minute before Robert motioned for another agent to open the door. It was locked, but the agent quickly picked it and they entered.

A few minutes later, they concluded that the senator was not in the house. He probably hadn't even been there at all, since there was no trace of him. Someone else though had obviously left in a hurry, because there was still lukewarm coffee standing on the kitchen table. Marsden carefully picked up the mug, wearing thin latex gloves, and examined it for a moment. There were distinct lipstick marks on it. So it was most likely the senator's wife who had left in such a hurry. Interesting. They continued to search the house through the night, but when morning came, they had to report back that there didn't seem to be any clues that would lead to anything. Nothing obvious at least, and with the Exodus almost ready to leave, time was working against them.

Later that day, FBI Director Barron made a call from his encrypted satellite phone to the head of the Consortium. He had been on the payroll of Havelar Industries for years, covertly of course, and while serving two masters would normally lead to conflicts of interest, serving both Havelar and the government seemed no different to Barron. He knew how closely entwined the president was in Consortium business, and as an inherently cautious man, he had taken his precautions. So if there ever were a problem, the president would never be able to pin him down unless he was willing to commit political suicide. George Havelar, who was now on board the Exodus, having secured a seat for himself and his closest associates, answered within seconds. Barron spoke in a low voice, even though there was no reason for it.

"It seems our sources were correct, the conspiracy is for real, and more than likely you have one or more traitors up there. We still suspect sabotage; there is a real danger that someone may be planning to harm the Exodus en route. Another possibility is assassination, which would make you a prime target. There may be other motives too, we really cannot say. I'm assuming you have several security measures in place?"

"Of course, Director," Havelar answered in a gruff voice. Ever the foresighted man, Havelar had probably predicted opposition from the beginning.

"And you do understand that I will not discuss them, right?" he continued.

"Certainly. Just make sure you've got your eyes and ears open." Havelar surprised Barron a little when he chuckled softly.

"Oh don't worry, Director. I have many eyes and ears. And they are ever watchful."

Chapter 10

February 2080 ~ Earth orbit

Tina Hammer eyed her new distinctions; major now. It didn't mean as much to her as it once had, but she still considered it a sign of the confidence entrusted upon her by the admiral. As second in command, she was expected to hold a higher rank. Admiral Hamilton had picked her himself, and she had been surprised. After all, she'd only been a captain, and she had expected a middling position on Exodus. She hadn't even been sure she'd be selected at all. But here she was, entrusted with command of the greatest achievement in human history, second only to the admiral himself.

Considering they were now finally orbiting Earth, she felt immensely proud. The feat accomplished in less than seven years was nothing short of amazing, but she also knew the price that had been paid. While almost every part of the Exodus was built on Earth, orbital assembly had been a massive project, and the safety regulations that would have been mandatory on any ordinary construction site had been virtually nonexistent for the assembly workers in space. There had been several bad injuries and even a few losses. A few unlucky workers were actually floating lifeless through space somewhere right now, while Tina was taking in the view of Earth from the bridge of the Exodus. The cost, in both monetary and human terms, had been astronomical, but the starship was ready, and the 1,628 crew and passengers were soon to leave on their final journey into deep space. This was the day they had been waiting for, the day the greatest adventure in human history would begin. She thought of her own journey so far, which had taken her through every obstacle the instructors had been able to throw at her, and even close to the front lines of a civil war, and she felt grateful. She knew that her own efforts and dedication had played a great part, but there had been a substantial element of luck involved. She was one of the very few who were given a chance for a new life on a distant world, and she felt that there were so many others who deserved it more. That's one of the reasons she'd stood up for the children from the last shuttle, and that was why she was so determined that every single person on board would be given the same chance to see the new world and build their new life there. The idea of sending the kids from the last shuttle back to Earth had made her stomach twist, and she would do whatever it took to avoid that. It seemed now, that with the plan for keeping a small part of the crew awake at all times, that could be avoided. And as an added bonus, they could get so much work done while in transit. Of course there would still be a while before anyone could be put to sleep, as the cryo cells needed adjustment, and there was still a lot of other work to be done. But in a couple of months, the first passengers would be put to sleep, and several of them wouldn't be revived at all before they reached Aurora, 165 years from now.

The Exodus was the pinnacle of human engineering and adaptability, and the designers had made redundancy, ease of maintenance, and speedy assembly the ruling guidelines in every aspect of its construction. And the time from decision to execution had been nothing short of a sensation. Humanity had shown that it actually did possess the ability to build a starship. When they discussed it, a lot of people wondered why it hadn't been done before. The media, slowly realizing their limitations within the current system, had started asking difficult questions, and down on Earth, the president was under a lot of pressure. The what-ifs of space exploration had suddenly become a major debate. Observers and opinion makers had started asking the questions that everyone asked themselves now that Earth was in dire peril. What if NASA hadn't been disbanded? What if this kind of ingenuity, combined with government support, had surfaced earlier? What if ten such voyages could have already colonized other planets? What if humanity hadn't been

Earthbound, and hence fragile and vulnerable in the face of such threats as Devastator? The answers seemed to be multiple. Lack of visionary leadership, the priority of immediate needs before long-term planning, control issues due to the impossibility of Earth's leadership to fully control a colony light years away, inability to plan for projects across generations, inability to fully realize the risk inherent in having all eggs in one basket. Tina had thought about all these things, and even discussed them with some of the others on board, such as Kenneth Taylor, whom she'd gotten acquainted with just a few weeks ago. Tina had been put in charge of the practical issues associated with reviving certain members of the crew throughout the duration of the journey, and thought it wise to consult with the psychologist on board. Although there would be a certain psychological strain involved in the periods of wakefulness on a large ship traveling through space, while most others would be asleep, the thing that concerned Tina the most was the waking process. From the experiments conducted on Earth, she'd learned that a percentage of those who were revived were prone to several afflictions, such as depression, despair, disorientation that could last for weeks, and in more rare cases even psychosis. It seemed there was something in the waking process that caused all this, although they couldn't be certain. But because they were going to have a lot of people experiencing that traumatic event—twice, they needed to do something about it. Taylor had offered some great advice on it, which would now be possible to implement, given the time at their disposal.

She had also discussed her thoughts on why man hadn't journeyed into deep space before with her long time friend Henry Carroll, who apparently had also given it a lot of thought. Henry, though, had come to different conclusions, and explained that what seemed so feasible now, would have been almost impossible to imagine with any degree of realism only a few years ago, when everything about the situation had been so different. From her discussions with Dr. Taylor and Henry, she had adjusted her views quite a bit. While sending a starship on an interstellar journey was something that could be done now, it had been very different in the years prior to the arrival of Devastator.

The truth was that any earlier starship would have been fundamentally different from the Exodus. There were three things that made the Exodus groundbreaking, in addition to its size and purpose. First, there was the fusion rocket, which enabled it to reach 5 percent of light speed. Combined with a gravity assist, a technique that had been used both in manned and unmanned spaceflight for a long time, and which basically meant sending the ship through a slingshot maneuver by the sun that actually doubled its speed, the fusion rocket was able to achieve 10 percent of light speed. Any attempt at sending a starship into deep space, utilizing either chemical propulsion or nuclear fission, would have been a lot slower, and the journey would have taken thousands of years. Nuclear fusion though, would have been the least of the problems, since the theory had been established and fusion reactors had actually been around for decades, but without a strong incentive, that had been as far as fusion technology had gone, until the need made further development imperative.

Second, the development of the modern cryogenic technique made the journey possible within the lifetime of its participants. Cryo sleep, or just Sleep, as it had come to be called among the inhabitants of the Exodus, was a technique that combined the old idea of lowering body temperature to slow down metabolism with newer developments that utilized chemicals to achieve and enhance the same purpose. That combination would, according to the scientists, prevent expansion of the cells due to lower temperatures and thus deterioration of the body, which had been one of the main concerns associated with the technique. The various stages of development had been tested on humans, and although very little information had come out of the labs, it was known that there had been losses and human suffering that would have been unbearable for a truly democratic society. Such a practice had been impossible to defend in public before the reforms. Even under the Andrews presidency and in the face of a threat to the survival of mankind, the inhuman aspects of such a practice had made the research and development of the technique one of the most guarded secrets of the government. But being able to put the participants on a journey of this scale to sleep, and to revive them again once they reached their destination, without their bodies having aged more than just a few months, made such a journey more likely to succeed for two reasons: first, the ones entering the ship to leave Earth would know that they would wake up to take part in the exploration and colonization of a new world. That would ensure that a sense of purpose could be preserved, and not be diluted and even lost throughout the ages. That was a very real possibility if the journey was to be undertaken by a generation ship, where the original spacefarers raised new generations on board, and those who reached their destination would have no personal relationship to Earth. Second, mastery of the cryogenic technique also made construction easier, because those asleep would need very little in the way of supplies, compared to an awake human being, and they could be stowed in their cryo cells, much like cargo containers on an ocean-going ship. That made the ship more economical in terms of volume. There would also be much less need for living quarters, although some living space had to be allowed for, not only for the crew, but because there would be periods at the start and the end of the journey when all would be awake. But for such limited periods, crowding and very little personal space would be more acceptable.

Third, the discovery of Nemesis. As the ESA had confirmed during the early brainstorming, Nemesis could serve as the key to decreasing the travel time from several millennia—clearly not an option—to just 165 years, which would feel like 161 to those on board, due to the time dilution effect caused by relativity. Without the existence—and discovery—of Nemesis, it would have taken more than four centuries to reach Aurora.

So any earlier attempts at colonizing other star systems would have taken a lot longer, and it would most likely have had to be undertaken by generation ships. It would have been possible, but both the technical and psychological aspects would have been vastly different.

Tina had only a few minutes before she had to join Admiral Hamilton for the final preparations for the initial boost that would take them out of Earth orbit. As her eyes took in this magnificent image of Earth, she realized that this was an entirely new stage of human development. They were being sent on a journey through space, to colonize and create a new life for human kind, and in the process they had learned to master interstellar travel. Although their new lives on Aurora would initially be a fight for survival, and primarily revolve around the exploration of a new planet for a long time, eventually they would want to explore even more. They would remember what happened to Earth, and there would be a drive to reach further, to find new worlds on which to plant the seeds of humanity. By then, they would have the means to do so, which meant that mankind would never again be as vulnerable as it was at this time. The thought comforted her, as she turned away from the view of Earth, so undisturbed and peaceful from this distance, and recognized she had seen her home world for the last time.

September 2080 ~ Solar system

There was really nothing remarkable about Thomas Dunn, no obvious reason for anyone to consider him an asset, but somehow he'd been able to convince George Havelar and the rest of the Consortium during those last few weeks before the launches began, that they needed to bring him along. He had none of the obvious skills required: he'd flunked out of college in his sophomore year, he had no military background, no medical skills, no craftsmanship or technical background, although he was handy enough, and of course he was not one of the lucky few who'd been able to buy their ticket off Earth. When asked about his role in the venture, he'd either shrug it away, or give some vague reference to colony management or personnel, but hardly anyone could actually say what his job would be once they reached the new world. His official title was junior executive, which of course meant absolutely nothing to anyone. Anyone except Havelar and a select few of the head figures on the Consortium, that was.

Before he approached Havelar's people the first time, Dunn had gotten his hands on a detailed description of the selection process out west, and he instantly knew that he wouldn't stand a chance going that route. So he had devised a plan that involved quite a bit of risk, and also a sacrifice; but the gains outweighed the risks, so he went through with it. He had his doubts about the sacrifice, but he'd pushed them out of his mind. He had, with the assistance of some very talented people, been given an entirely new identity, and his old life had been completely erased. The old Thomas Dunn, or whatever his name might have been, existed only in his own private memories now. When Havelar, or anyone else for that matter, did a background check on him, they would find that he'd been involved in some shady business in Europe, involving an attempted overthrow of the mainly socialist government of Greece, and had barely escaped the authorities there, before settling for a while in Turkey, running a restaurant business. From time to time his name would appear in reports pertaining to several arms dealers and security service providers in the Middle East and Africa, although he never seemed to have a prominent role, and there seemed to be no active participation on his part. Then, during the civil war, his name would pop up in connection with Istanbul intelligence. Of course, that could never be completely verified, since all intelligence records had been burned before the fall of Istanbul, and those who could be connected to his name had fallen or disappeared during those last chaotic days of the regime. Thomas Dunn had then turned up at Miami International Airport six months later with a forged French passport and been detained briefly, until the authorities had finally bought into his explanation that he'd had to get a fake passport to get out of Turkey alive. He'd been charged, but released with a suspended sentence for carrying forged documents to gain access onto American soil.

When he'd contacted Havelar's people, they had immediately checked up on him, once he offered information on a conspiracy against the Exodus project. He'd told them that he'd been approached by an Englishman who had known ties to terrorist financiers, a man that only existed on paper, of course. This man had, according to his story, said he could get him into the selection process for the Exodus. His role then would be to send information out through an associate, who happened to work for the Energy Department. The reason he'd been approached, he was told, was his reputation for being a professional and utterly mercenary. And although he'd been involved in a lot of dirty business in the cause of good money, he was also a true patriot, so he'd considered going to the police with this information. But then it had occurred to him that there was another way to go about this. So he'd decided to go to the Consortium with the information, on one condition; that they got him on board the Exodus. In return he would smoke out the conspiracy, get to know the people who could be involved, and use his knowledge to infiltrate and subvert the conspiracy from within. After a few initial meetings with Consortium security officers, he'd been given an audience with the man himself, George Havelar. At that point he knew that they had bought into his story. But there were even bigger schemes at work, and with his seat on board the Exodus secured, his next move could be made.

He was late for his meeting with Havelar, but he saw no reason to rush it. His cool, unconcerned demeanor was all part of his persona, part of who Thomas Dunn was. So he walked with a slow pace through the corridors, while thinking how convenient the artificial gravity was, to a person like him, who had worried how the lack of gravity would affect his way of behaving; whether he would be able to keep up the whole charade. One less thing to worry about, he thought to himself. He came around a corner and almost bumped into a man he seemed to recognize.

"Ah, Kenneth Taylor, right? The shrink?" He winked.

The psychologist smiled back and replied. "That's right, ah, Mr. Dunn?" Thomas nodded quickly. So he's noticed me, he thought.

"So what are you up to, Mr. Dunn? One last glimpse of Earth? We should be able to see it by now," Taylor continued. After the gravity assist by the sun they were now passing Earth one last time on their journey through the solar system.

"Nah, just getting some exercise." As Thomas heard his own words, he heard how lame they sounded. He was a fit young man; walking wasn't what he'd consider exercise.

"Well, that's important, I guess. Or, it used to be, back when I was a space cadet." Now that was interesting. The shrink had been a space cadet? He'd never have guessed. Maybe there was more to the old brain tinkerer than he let on. He'd have to check up on that.

"I didn't know you were a space cadet," Thomas said. The psychologist just smiled.

"Well, maybe I'll tell you the story later, over a beer. Say, in 165 years perhaps?" They both laughed politely, and then carried on in opposite directions. Thomas continued toward the rear of the living quarters area, where the Consortium held a small compartment that Havelar normally had reserved to himself. As Dunn reached the door, he paused to gather his thoughts.

His cover story was a mix of details, a lot of them true, others convenient little half truths and lies that fit the mix and the purpose of his story. Of course, the picture he'd painted to Havelar and his goons wasn't even remotely close to the truth about who Thomas Dunn really was.

He knew that the stakes were high, and that he, just as every other individual involved, was expendable. The greater good was the important thing, and as long as the main objective was preserved, that justified all sacrifices. After all, this was about the future of mankind, and what mankind would become. So, for the greater good, he had condemned a poor Energy Department employee to torture, using him as bait to gain the confidence of his enemies. That had further led to the death of a great man, as dedicated to the cause as he was. He had only met him once, but the man had impressed him with his vision, his long-term planning, and his ability to get results without the FBI suspecting anything. Thatcher, he recalled, had been one of the masterminds behind the plan, and so he must have known that his own fate would be sealed. Now even the senator was a wanted man. Dunn could only hope that he'd get away, although it didn't seem likely. America was a police state these days, and to disappear from the eyes of the powerful FBI took considerable resources, lots of planning, and preferably help from the inside.

Others too would be sacrificed, and when he thought about that, he remembered a quote from Nietzsche: "Battle not with monsters, lest ye become a monster, and if you gaze into the abyss, the abyss gazes also into you." Every time he thought of that quote, and he had done so frequently of late, he got a feeling he was balancing on a knife's edge, and that the abyss was reaching up for him.

As he entered the room, the question still remained: who was Thomas Dunn?

Chapter 11

October 2084 ~ Somewhere in Arizona

The days seemed endless, and most days were the same. There were no assignments, nothing to do, and nothing to help pass the time. Most importantly, there was to be no contact with the outside world. John Rawlins had no idea how many there were, as they were divided into barracks, and there was no way to tell how many barracks there were. The guards kept a close eye on them, and John had seen what would happen if they suspected someone to be a troublemaker. There were a few guards who were obviously uncomfortable in their guard roles, and they would at times be all right, even sympathetic, but most had adapted to the role disturbingly well. As a former soldier, John felt ashamed at what these young troops could make themselves do. He had never thought he'd see young American men and women turn into something like this. He knew all too well that murder had become commonplace, and even lesser offenses would bring harsh punishment. Trying to escape was punishable by death. That had been mistaken for a bad joke at first, he'd heard from some who had been here longer than he. But, it soon became apparent, it was definitely no joke, and he'd seen a few of the executions himself. And then it was the mass punishments. If one person did something the guards deemed wrong, like trying to steal food or trying to get information from the guards, the entire barracks would be punished. The punishments would range from denial of food or having to stand in line out in the sun all day, to corporal punishment and executing such punishment on each other. In a few cases, the guards had chosen an entire barracks and made them march until one succumbed to fatigue. The poor fellow was then clubbed to death by other prisoners held at gunpoint. In all, detention had turned out to be a nightmare.

He had withdrawn from Selection when he'd learned the truth about Devastator to be with his family, who hadn't been lucky enough to be picked. He had said good-bye to Maria, Jeremiah, and the rest of his team, before taking his belongings with him and entering the bus leaving the compound. The bus was a regular shuttle that almost every day took those who were kicked out or voluntarily chose to throw in the towel, and he was told it would take him to the nearest town, which had a bus station. After twenty minutes, the bus had been stopped by a patrol of soldiers, and the driver had stepped out. It all seemed routine to him, but when the soldiers had ordered them to be quiet and sit still, as one of the soldiers took the wheel, he had felt a knot in his stomach. They had driven for three hours, when they saw the camp. There was barbed wire, a sign that read "minefield," and armed troops everywhere. They had driven through the gate, and were brusquely gathered in a group by soldiers. One guy had spoken up against their captors, and had been slammed to the ground with rifle butts, so the rest of them had meekly continued through the processing area. The soldiers had taken all personal belongings, and outfitted them with some sort of pajamas. Their shoes had been taken from them, to make escape more difficult, he suspected.

"What's for dinner tonight?" Johanna Peters asked. She was the one in his barracks who'd been here the longest, more than ten years now, having failed one of the first tests, back in '74. John admired her. She always had a comment that would bring a smile, and she seemed determined not to be taken by despair.

"Stew and stale bread, always stew and stale bread," a sullen voice said from the shadows. It was Derek Hewitt, once a renowned heart surgeon, now a depressed and broken man, who would go catatonic for days. John worried that he would either starve himself to death or make a desperate run for it, despite the consequences.

They were sitting outside the barracks, with nothing to do, and nothing to talk about, when John noticed that the guard that usually brought them food and water was running late. The soldiers were never late, at least he couldn't remember that ever happening, so he got up on his feet, and looked around the corner. It wasn't just that they were hungry, although that played a part, as food was always scarce. It was more the fact that they had become so used to the routine, that anything out of the ordinary immediately got their attention.

"Hmm, that's weird," he said. "I can't see any guards up in the tower." He shaded his eyes with his hand, squinting against the harsh sunlight. Then he noticed one of the other detainees running across the open courtyard, shouting something he couldn't make out. Johanna came over to him, and even Derek decided to get up.

"What the hell is going on?" Johanna said.

"I have no idea," John answered absently. "Where are the guards?" They looked at each other, puzzlement plain on their faces, and slowly walked over to where the man had run. All they could see was other detainees, but no guards. Now that John thought about it, there had been a lot of noise about an hour ago, maybe less, engines, shouted commands, and the like. Then the camp had gone mostly quiet. The detainees had for the most part stayed indoors, because the sun was too baking hot to be outdoors, but someone would have noticed what had happened.

"It seems they have all left," he said quietly. He didn't want to think about what that meant, but he knew he had to.

"That can only mean one thing: it's happening." As far as John could tell, the Exodus had left Earth orbit years ago. They had received no information while in detention, and could only guess at what was happening on the outside, but there were always rumors, and sometimes the guards would let something slip.

"Devastator is coming," Derek said, his face contorting into a grimace, a change from his usual blank expression which normally would be a welcome one. John eyed him sideways, then walked over to one of the other detainees to ask if they knew anything. A minute later, he came back to the others, and confirmed what they had just discussed.

"Eric from F Barracks says that the guards left a while ago, and left the gate open. He says he talked to a friendly guard who told him they were ordered up north in a hurry."

"Is it the rebellion they were talking about?" Johanna asked.

"No, this is something else. He said the guard told him that last rebellion fizzled out as soon as the launches were complete, back in '79, but now there seems to be a new war going on up in Idaho and Montana. It's supposed to have gone nuclear, and it's spreading fast."

"Oh shit, that's all we need now," Johanna said. Derek, a few steps off, cringed at the news. He had family in Spokane, Washington, not far from the Idaho border. For a short while, they didn't speak, until John decided to take charge.

"Well, this changes things," he finally said.

"First of all, we need to get out of here. The stores won't last the day, when the word gets out. We're talking minutes before people will be pouring out of their barracks, and they will take everything they can get a hold of. It will be chaotic, to say the least.

"Second, we need to decide where to go. We don't know how destructive Devastator will be, but we know it will be bad. Where do we want to be when it comes?" He seemed to draw inward for a moment, then spoke again.

"I left Selection to be with my family. For me the choice is simple, I'm going north. Boulder, Colorado is where

I'll be heading. You're welcome to tag along if you want, as long as you remember that reaching them is my priority."

"I'm with you, John," Derek said. He smiled, a sad smile that somehow seemed to convey acceptance or maybe it was resignation. "My wife lives in LA, but we were separated just before I left for Selection. She's better off without me. I have no kids, and there's no way I'll be able to get all the way to my relatives up in Spokane before Devastator gets here. It's not like getting a plane ticket these days, you know." He shuffled his feet, looking down, then spread his hands and peered out toward the gate.

"Like I said, I'm with you, John. I'll help you find your family. Too many bad things have happened here, and I for one would like to see something good happen for a change."

"Amen to that," Johanna followed. "I have no family left here. My sister Tori came with me to Selection, and I haven't seen her since. She's probably somewhere in space now. She was always the serious one, while I was the goofball that managed to be kicked out after the first test." She laughed softly, while nodding to herself. "So I'm with you as well." John smiled at the two of them, his closest friends since he'd been detained, with whom he'd shared so much.

"All right. Then let's hurry up, and get moving. We need to get some provisions, then get out of here as soon as possible."

They hurried over to the guards' quarters, where a few other detainees had already turned up and started looting. Then they spent a few minutes filling a couple of bags with canned and dried food, some clothes, a wristwatch, a map and compass, and some other supplies they figured would be handy. All the while, more people came in, as the news spread, and as soon as their bags were filled, they hurried out through the gate.

They followed the road north the rest of the day, and when night fell, they camped near a small brook, just a trickle really, although normally it should be a wide river this time of year. The night was cooler than expected, but they had brought blankets, and they had a fire going, and all in all it felt good to be out here in the open. The feeling of freedom was something John had learned to appreciate early in life, and this reminded him of some of his hiking trips during his youth. He had always been an outdoorsman, which had been an asset when he joined the army straight out of high school. Then, after six years, he'd traded his army fatigues for a civilian life, and gone to college to study engineering. That's when he'd met Melissa. She'd been a bright young engineering student, and although she was several years younger than he, they'd hit it off at once, and when they both graduated, they got married in her local church in Charlottesville, Virginia. Melissa had stayed at home with the kids for a few years, and the job market had been tough when she decided to start working again. So they had moved to Boulder five years ago, when she got a job there. John had it a little easier, with more experience and several projects on his résumé, so he landed the first job he applied for. Now, as the last of the fire gradually died out, he looked up at the stars, and he felt a yearning to be with his family that felt like it would tear him apart.

Whatever it takes, he thought to himself, as he vowed to be strong. He would take whatever came, and no matter what distance he had to walk, no matter the obstacles he would meet, he would never ever give up.

"I'll be with you again," he whispered softly to avoid being overheard by the others. "Whatever it takes."

November 2084 ~ Close to Cheyenne, Wyoming

Trevor Hayes sat in his holding cell in the FBI's High Security facility in Wyoming, waiting for his interrogators to show up. They should have been here by now, he thought. How long had it been since he came here, he thought, confused after weeks of hard interrogation. While still in his White House office, he had seen every person he knew to be involved in the conspiracy arrested and taken away, except the senator of course, who had disappeared before the Exodus left Earth orbit four years ago. They had never caught him, and Trevor wondered whether he was still alive, out there somewhere, hunted by every agency in the country. Then one day, as he was taking his daily morning run, he had received a phone call from President Andrews, still in office, in his fourth term. The president had simply told him he was disappointed, before he hung up. Moments later, several FBI agents had appeared and brusquely handcuffed him, before shoving him into a black van. He had been sedated, and when he came to he was here in this building. The interrogators had made his location no secret, and he knew it didn't matter. He knew of the place, and no one had ever escaped it. He also knew what the interrogators wanted, but they would never get what they sought, as he was unable to give them that information. Of course, telling them that didn't help. The interrogation sessions had been worse than he expected. Obviously, all pretense of being a democracy had vanished over the last couple of years, and although interrogation had always been a tough experience, especially when things like national security were said to be on the line, there had always been a distinction between interrogation and flat out torture. Not anymore though. Well, it didn't matter either. The interrogators had been clear that they wanted names. They had gotten the names of the conspirators on Earth a long time ago, it seemed, at least most of them. But the ones on the Exodus had, as far as he knew, never been exposed. And now they seemed desperate. That told him that it couldn't be long before impact.

The cell had no windows, so there was no way to know whether it was day or night, but he had the feeling it might be night, since the corridors seemed too quiet. There should have been sounds of footsteps, doors opening and closing, keys rattling. Unlike the interrogation cells, the holding cells weren't soundproof, so there was always some kind of noise. Now there was nothing. Since no interrogators seemed to show up, that gave Trevor the chance to think. Earth was apparently doomed, they knew that Devastator was coming, and soon. They didn't know where it would hit, and that was just as well. The effects would be global, and those who didn't die from the impact would most certainly die in the aftermath. Well, Trevor thought, at least those on the Exodus have a chance now. They will make a better world. Earth was a wreck anyhow, he thought. The slow transition into tyranny that had taken place in America was by no means unique. And the way things had been for the last fifty years, it was unlikely that Earth would have been able to cope much longer. Overpopulation, global warming, pollution. We destroyed what we were given, he thought. In the end, nature struck back. Of course, it wasn't that simple, but Trevor didn't care anymore. He needed simple. That was how he still held on to his sanity these days.

As he sat there, alone with his thoughts, he could suddenly feel deep tremors, and as the shaking intensified he was thrown to the floor. After a few seconds of dizziness, he got his wits back, and though he stayed on the floor, he looked around. The door had been twisted out of its frame, and as he crawled toward it, he saw that it was only connected to the frame by its hinges. The lock had been twisted open, and the door looked like it could actually be pushed out by force. He sat up, adrenaline surging through his body, and with his back against the door, he pushed as hard as he could with his feet. The door moved a bit, and he was able to crawl out. There was no one outside, and then he saw that the roof had collapsed at one end of the corridor. The other end looked unharmed, and Trevor got to his feet and went that way. Maybe, if he could just get out of the building … There was no telling how things looked on the outside, maybe it was as deserted as it was inside. Maybe he could actually escape? He continued a few steps before he was thrown to the floor by a second wave of tremors. The whole building shook, and there was a deep rumble that felt like it came closer. As he lay there, he realized the futility of what he was doing. There would be no escape from Devastator. Then the entire building started shaking, and parts of the roof fell down around him. The lights went out, and he called for help. He knew no one would hear him, but it still felt better doing something, rather than nothing. That was his last thought as the building collapsed on top of him.

November 2084 ~ Colorado Springs, Colorado

They had been walking for weeks, and by now they had reached the northern outskirts of Colorado Springs. It wouldn't be long until they reached Denver, and they had to decide whether to risk going through the city or take a detour around it. As far as anyone knew, they were still escaped detainees, and based on what little they'd been able to learn since they'd left the camp, there was very little left of the country they had once known and loved. There were police shooting people on mild suspicion of minor offenses, army personnel looting and taking whatever they could get their hands on, and the war raging on in the north had brought an endless stream of refugees southward. And Devastator was coming. The last few days and nights had been cloudy, so they hadn't seen it, but apparently they should've been able to if the weather had been clear. John Rawlins had begun to worry that they wouldn't make it to Boulder in time to be reunited with his family, but they were by no means on the verge of giving up.

Derek Hewitt had shown himself to be a resource, despite John's doubts when they set out on foot. It was remarkable what he knew, and he seemed to be able to scrounge together resources however sparse and turn them into something useful. Like the radio they now had, that allowed them to catch up on what was going on in the world. That was something Derek had fiddled with night after night by their camp fire, and within a week, they were able to listen to the news, some kind of music, and the occasional report from the starship Exodus, which by now had left the solar system altogether.

Johanna Peters on the other hand, had come down with a bad case of pneumonia, and Rawlins didn't know what to do for her. They couldn't see a doctor or get her to a hospital, and she seemed to weaken a little more every day. Without antibiotics, John worried that she might not survive their trek. Now, as they were preparing their camp for the night, John heard her coughing until she vomited. She had gone off behind some bushes for some private business, as she called it, but he suspected she also tried to hide how bad a condition she was actually in.

Suddenly, a flash of light appeared on the horizon to the west. At first it was bright white and lit up the twilight sky, then it slowly turned yellow, and after about a minute it became a deep orange glow, which didn't go away. A few minutes later the ground shook, and they were tossed around by tremors too violent to remain standing or even sitting. All the while there was a rumbling sound like thunder.

"Oh shit," Derek said, as the tremors slowly subsided. "Was that …" John nodded while gritting his teeth. It couldn't have been anything else. And soon they would feel the aftershocks and the other effects, whatever they might be. They had very little time, and if they were to survive, they would have to move quickly. They both looked around, and saw Johanna slowly come creeping out from the bushes. Her expression was twisted, and there was sweat in between the dirt on her face. Her face looked pale, and her eyes were half closed. She coughed and spat, and she moved slowly, crawling over the ground, every movement seemed to take an eternity. John immediately saw that there was something else, not just the pneumonia, although that was already bad enough. Then, as he ran over to her, he became aware of her left leg, and the way it twisted in an odd angle at her knee. There was blood pouring in regular spouts out of her broken knee, and now they could see the bone sticking out. Not a word came out of her mouth; she only coughed and gasped for air. Then their eyes met, and she slowly shook her head. He instantly knew that she wouldn't live long, and it seemed she understood as well. For a split second, he considered making a travois, an old Indian method for transportation, and dragging her along, but he knew there was no time. Johanna looked him in the eyes for a few seconds before she smiled faintly and closed her eyes.

Moments later, it seemed like an eternity to John, Derek came over. He touched John on the shoulder and whispered, as if afraid that someone might hear his words.

"We need to get going. She would have wanted us to."

She's not dead, John wanted to call out, a sudden flash of anger at them both, but his words caught in his throat. He knew Derek was right, and that Johanna would have wanted them to carry on. She still breathed, although wheezing and laboriously, but he knew it wouldn't be long until she stopped breathing altogether. They slowly stood up beside their dying companion. Neither of them said anything as they looked toward the light on the western horizon. Finally Derek went over to where their bags and equipment lay scattered on the ground and started filling the bags with whatever he deemed worth carrying. They knew the aftershocks were probably just minutes away, but they couldn't sit still anymore. John walked over and started helping out. They carelessly stuffed their bags until they couldn't fit anything more. As soon as they had packed as much as they could carry, they looked at each other, then cast a final look at Johanna, who still seemed to breathe faintly, and started walking. John realized they would probably be dead soon. But better to die walking toward something, than while hiding out in a hole somewhere. Devastator had finally struck, and there was nowhere to hide from that.

Chapter 12

2086 ~ Interstellar space

More than six years had passed since the Exodus left Earth orbit. Since then, the starship had first traveled inward for the slingshot by the sun, before it passed through the solar system at 10 percent of light speed on its way toward Nemesis. Four years into the journey, they had received a final signal, before Earth went absolutely quiet. That had been just hours after the projected impact by Devastator, and considering the time it took for the transmission to reach them, it would have been recorded some time before or after the impact itself. No one would ever know what happened to their home world, now that it had gone quiet.

The Exodus had continued its journey, undisturbed, through the vast emptiness of space beyond the solar system, following the carefully plotted course through the Oort Cloud. Reaching the twin star of the sun, the starship had made a second slingshot, before finally reaching cruise velocity. The fusion rocket had been spent when accelerating toward the sun, and after two slingshot maneuvers the starship now floated through space at more than a quarter of light speed, on a steady course toward Aurora. Before it reached its destination, the magnetic sails, now stowed in the nose of the ship, would fold out and give it the deceleration it would need in order to enter an orbit around the new world.

Tina Hammer hadn't been around for any of this, having been deep in Sleep since before the first gravity assist by the sun. Waking had been a terrible experience, from which she was still recovering, and she could understand perfectly well why something had to be done about the process. It had been three days, and still she felt feverish. The price you pay for survival, she thought to herself. She'd been through rough times before though, so she knew it would pass. In a couple of weeks, the guinea pigs, as she'd come to think of them, would be revived the second time around. She would have to steel herself for that. She knew that if they were physically damaged by being subjected to cryo sleep twice, she would have a nasty task ahead of her. She could hope for the best, but in the worst-case scenario, she would have to be quick and ruthless. That would be the only way to save the rest of the crew and passengers of the Exodus from the same fate. There simply weren't enough cryo cells to let everyone sleep through the entire journey, which had always been deemed the safest option. That had been the plan all along, and the ship had even been outfitted with ten extra cells just to have spares in case of a failure. They had also thought these could be used for parts, in case an emergency

216

repair had to be done. In such a case, the repairs could have been performed by the maintenance robots, or bots as they were called among the inhabitants on the Exodus. But even the best laid plans cannot predict every conceivable event, and when a shuttle filled with children was launched up from the wreckage of a civil war, the commander of the Exodus, Admiral Greg Hamilton, had conceded to try every effort to save everyone on board. The responsibility for making sure this didn't cause them injury—or worse—all had fallen on Tina, and she would have to deal with the consequences if their method failed.

For the next two weeks, Tina got up to speed with what had happened so far, reading and studying about the trip and going over the news from Earth until it went silent. Although the thought of what would most likely have happened back on Earth saddened her, she'd accepted it and dealt with all that a long time ago. Humanity was now right here on this ship, and would continue to live on and prosper once they settled in on their new home. Having no family to leave behind back on Earth probably helped her establish such perspective. She also spent considerable time reviewing the data from the last waking of the guinea pigs. Although there was nothing spectacular or remarkable about these data, she knew she'd have to make thorough comparisons, and she needed to know exactly how to spot anomalies that might indicate that something was wrong, and separate those from variations that would be considered normal. There were fifteen others awake at the time, but none of them were initiated into this; they were computer technicians and life-support technicians, and a few scientists, such as Karin Svensson, the ESA astronomer. Tina needed to make sure that her decisions were correct, or she'd endanger the entire ship and all of its inhabitants. In Selection, she'd studied medicine, so she had already familiarized herself with the terminology, and if she could only find the key data that would indicate anomalies, this task should be something she could perform with a level of certainty.

When the day came, Tina had prepared herself for whatever would come. She would start by reviving one, then go through all the tests and evaluate the data she got, and at last compare it to the data from the last time that person was awake. It was a tedious process, and would most likely take the entire day. If there was something wrong, and that proved to be serious enough, she would make sure that when she revived the next person that would be the first thing to look for. In all, she would have to wake up at least three people to be certain. If there was a system to it, a recognizable pattern, she would execute her contingency plan. She would fake a small radioactive leak, and give everyone awake, including the scientists and technicians an iodine pill that had the side effect of putting them sound asleep, and then she would inject a lethal dose of morphine. Instead of reviving the others, she would let them sleep. That would minimize the losses to only those who'd actually been woken twice. All this would be properly logged, and she would finish a report that would document everything that had been done, the findings that she had made, and how all of this had been done to ensure the survival of as many as possible. Then she would check the settings for each and every cryo cell, so that no others would be woken before the ship reached Aurora. In the end, she would inject the last dose into her own vein. That wasn't part of the plan she'd discussed with Admiral Hamilton, but there were some things that shouldn't be discussed with anyone. She would share the fate of those she had condemned, that much she would decide for herself.

The first person to wake up from cryo sleep was a young administrative assistant. Her name was Tori Peters, a blonde around thirty, although with her shaven head and distorted features from the agony of waking, Tina thought she looked at least forty. As she tried to comfort her while she sobbed and shivered, she quickly took blood and skin samples for testing. Then, after about an hour, Tori calmed and, although feverish and somewhat disoriented, she was able to take care of herself, so Tina went back to the lab to get the samples analyzed. That would take hours, so as soon as she had placed the samples in the appropriate slots, she went to get Tori a cup of nice Darjeeling tea.

"D ... did it feel like this for you as well?" she asked. Tina just smiled at her while she nodded.

"I d ... didn't remember how bad it was ... But I ... guess it was the same the last time ..." Her teeth rattled and she shivered hard. Tina didn't know whether she should get to know the guinea pigs, or whether it would be wise to avoid them just in case. After a moment of hesitation, she decided that she couldn't get all the data she needed just from samples. The psychological effects might not show if she didn't try to get to know them. Her conversations with the ship's psychologist, Kenneth Taylor, had made her realize that even if the physical samples turned up nothing, there might be damage that only a close examination of the psychological state of those who were woken would expose, such as certain brain damages. There might be long-term effects that would take years to expose, but that was something that Taylor had thought could be mended with the proper treatment, so it shouldn't condemn anyone to death. Tina decided to get to know them as well as possible. She knew she would be able to perform her duties if need be; it was something her military background had taught her. To save many lives, you sometimes had to make sacrifices. And the personal pain you felt when you knew those who would be sacrificed, or even when you had to make the hard decisions of who would live and who would die, was just as much a part of the sacrifice.

"Waking up from this is probably the worst thing I've ever been through," she said quietly. "But it heals, just give it time." She smiled reassuringly, while Tori sipped her tea. She had difficulty holding the cup steady, and spilled hot tea over her fingers, so Tina took the cup from her hands and held it carefully up to her lips. Tori smiled faintly and gave her a grateful look. As she finished her tea, Tina left her alone for a while and went back to the lab to wait for the first round of results.

Three days later, she had woken four people, and still she had found nothing to indicate that waking more than once had any lasting effects, other than the short-term agony and distress experienced by the process itself. As she went over the results one final time, she let out a breath of relief. She then took out her tablet to start filing her report. She now felt certain they could get everyone on board safely to Aurora. Eventually her report would be publicly known, and everyone would know what would have happened in the event waking more than once had been deemed dangerous. There would be a lot of questions, she knew that. But in the end, she also knew the hard truth of it all. Her primary goal had been to get everyone safely to the new world, and so far it had been a success.

It had been more than a century since the Exodus left Earth with its more than sixteen hundred inhabitants, but decades still remained. Kenneth Taylor had been awake for almost a year now, and still had more than a year left until he was to be put back to Sleep. He had worried about the possible danger of multiple Sleep cycles, but studying Tina Hammer's report from her investigation a century ago had reassured him that the only effects were the possible psychological trauma experienced during the waking process. And several scientists were working on designing a better way. As one scientist would finish part of the research necessary, another would pick up when the first went back to Sleep. Kenneth was one of those, and his main propositions for those who followed would be to create an environment that made the subjects feel like they were waking up in the morning, from natural sleep. Others would research the possibility of using a cocktail of various drugs to induce a feeling of well-being, postponing consciousness until the worst physical effects had subsided, and so on. Having extensive research experience, he felt they were making better progress than what he was used to from his own career back on Earth. He supposed that was due to the ability to work with very little distraction for a two-year period, and then leave the work for someone else, who would then go at it with a new perspective and new energy. This made everyone work faster individually, as the time limit was fixed. At the same time, the many heads working on the same problem ensured that every angle was covered, which provided a quality rarely found in Earth-based science. As a matter of fact, Kenneth thought they had accidentally discovered an entirely different way of conducting science, which felt deeply satisfying. In a few cycles, the research phase would come to an end, and the engineers and technicians would take over. He was curious as to how they would be able to use the insights gained from all those years of research to tweak the waking process into something better. He shrugged. There was nothing else to do but wait and see how it would be once they reached Aurora.

Even though his task at hand occupied his mind most of the time, there were times when he'd put his research aside, and contemplate something that had bothered him ever since they left Earth orbit. It would creep up from the back of his mind; a mystery he couldn't seem to solve properly, and once it came over him, he couldn't shake the feeling, even now. Back on Earth there had been a lot of arrests, both before and after launch. So many people had been revealed as having been part of a conspiracy connected to Project

Exodus. Even the director, Senator Buchanan, had been one of the conspirators, and rumors had it there might even be conspirators on board. In the early days, there was talk of sabotage, but now that they had travelled so far, he for one didn't believe that anymore. There had to be something else, but what? And the thing that really made him wonder was the fact that no one, as far as he knew, had been arrested aboard the Exodus. If the director had been involved, surely there had to be someone on the Exodus itself.

Having mused over the possibilities during this past year, privately, of course, since such matters weren't discussed openly, he had come to his own conclusion that there was no plan to disrupt or sabotage anything. What purpose would be served at this point? But his presence on the ship was puzzling. In Andrews's America, he wouldn't normally have stood a chance of being among the few selected for such a journey as this. Even though he'd never been vocal when it came to his political views, in a society governed by the fear of real and imagined enemies, he knew it was naïve to think that he'd escaped being monitored by the ever-present eyes and ears of the government. And, that being the case, why would someone with views contrary to the current administration's be selected? The only possible answer he could envision was that someone had gone to a lot of trouble to make sure that critical voices and dissidents were allowed on board. The goal of that might actually be to make sure the values and principles that had been gradually torn apart after Mars and Seattle would be brought back to life on the new world. That would surely have meant that even more people in the security services, the FBI, and the project had to be involved. And it definitely had to mean that someone close to Havelar, who had been appointed by the president to become acting governor as soon as they established themselves on Aurora, would have to be involved too, in order to divert attention from such people even after the starship left Earth. But who? It was impossible to know for sure. Besides, he had already decided to leave these things be for the time being. After all, if he was right, someone was protecting him and others, to make sure they made it safely to the new world. And what if he did discover who that someone was? If he dug too deeply into this, he might end up helping those who would rather see the new world populated with obedient conformists; to build a world in the image of Havelar and Andrews. No, he would keep his thoughts to himself. He would do as he'd done for so many years back on Earth; observe and keep his mouth shut.

The alarm sounded throughout the ship, loud enough to hear, but not so loud that people would be unable to focus or concentrate on their immediate tasks. Kenneth Taylor started as he heard the sound, and immediately left the lounge compartment where he'd been relaxing after having too large a dinner with a couple of the others. He quickly ran over to the console by the door and saw that this was something he should stay out of. There were already technicians working on the problem, and although the maintenance bots were capable of dealing with all sorts of situations, he felt more reassured knowing there were actual humans around who had the insight and knowledge to handle this.

The door closed automatically as he stood there; a safety precaution in case of a hull breach. That way, if they lost one compartment the others would hold, and losses would be minimized. He sat down again, took out his tablet, and logged on to the open comms channel, where he could follow the crisis as it unfolded. In deep space there was very little that could interfere with the starship, but one of the things they had occasionally seen were meteors. He had no idea where they came from, or whether they orbited some distant star or were rogues such as the planet that had hit Mars. But they were out there, and in this instance, it seemed the ship had come too close to a meteor tail, where microscopic pieces of debris had hit the ship. Although the pieces were small, the speed of both the comet and the

Exodus meant they hit with tremendous force, causing damages much larger than their size would imply. According to one of the technicians, speaking rapidly as she checked the status of each and every compartment, there were two breached hulls, the thing they feared the most. The lesser damages would be taken care of by the bots, with no need for human intervention. However, there was a fist-sized hole in the stowed magnetic sail, which would require one of the human technicians to inspect it before deciding what to do with it. Normally that would be an easy fix by the bots, but there was a danger of damaging the sail even more, so a human would have to make a decision whether to leave it as it was or to attempt a repair.

Kenneth listened intently as he followed the progress of the men and women working the problem, and as helpless as he was, locked in his sealed compartment with no way to be of any assistance, he knew the technicians were capable and resourceful. Half an hour later, one of them was space walking outside, tethered to the ship by a long wire. He had to get past several cargo compartments before he could access the shield behind which the magnetic sail was stowed. But just as he located the hole, the wire that tethered him got stuck. He could see that the hole was bigger than they had thought, and that it needed immediate repair, otherwise it would widen and the entire sail would be jeopardized. Without the magnetic sail, the ship would be unable to decelerate enough to enter Aurora orbit, and they risked overshooting the planet, with no way to turn the starship around. The technician discussed it with the on-board team for maybe a minute, and it was decided he had to perform a manual repair as soon as possible. Indeed, this was a perilous situation, made more so because the technician had to unhook himself from the tether in order to reach and repair the hole. He had to be sure to maintain physical contact with the ship at all times, or risk being adrift in space with no hope of rescue. There would be no second chances, should he slip or lose his grip. Kenneth's eyes were fixed on his screen, watching the technician slowly and very carefully proceed, creeping along the ship's hull toward the hole. When he reached it, he immediately started repairing the damage with spares he'd carried along in a bag fixed to his EVA suit.

"All right, it's done. Returning to airlock," Kenneth heard the technician say. He let out a relieved breath. The danger was passed, and unless there were more incidents like this one, they should be safe until they reached Aurora. Just as he was about to put his tablet away, he heard loud, excited voices on the speaker, and he looked at his tablet again. It seemed the technician had forgotten to latch onto the wire

229

again, and had slipped as he was creeping along the hull toward the airlock. Now he was floating away from the ship, and fast.

"We'll get you, Vinnie. Just hang on," he heard someone say. There was a moment of silence, before he heard the technician, Vinnie, again.

"Forget it, guys. You won't get to me in time. I'm already a hundred meters out. In thirty seconds, it'll be more than two hundred. It's going too fast. I don't want you to risk it." Kenneth thought he understood what Vinnie was talking about. He was caught up in an outward motion and gaining speed. There was no way that the others would get a wire to him, simply because the wire would soon be moving slower than he was. He was lost, and he knew it. The amazing thing was that he was so calm about it, Kenneth thought. He wondered whether it was heroism or fatalism. But whatever it was, somehow, in a bizarre way, he thought the dying man's acceptance of his fate was admirable.

Secured to the outside of one of the cargo compartments, there were four large containers. They were insulated and deftly hidden from anyone inspecting the ship, either manually or using the bots. A decade ago, there had been an incident, in which one man had died, where the starship had gotten too close to a meteor tail. The hole that the now-deceased technician had repaired had been on the outer layer of the forward compartment, where the magnetic sail was stowed. The four containers were located right behind where the hole had been, and the technician had actually been crawling across them, without noticing the oddness of having containers secured to the outside, instead of having them safely stowed within the ordinary cargo containers. Thomas Dunn shook his head at the thought. Of course, the technician had probably been too busy to notice, or too busy to report the thing. Whatever the reason, the containers remained hidden.

Besides being out of sight, the containers officially weren't even on board. They were nowhere to be found on the cargo manifest, and just a few people knew they were even there. Even fewer knew what they contained. Even Thomas, having been part of smuggling them on board, didn't know exactly what they held, but he could think of a few things, and none of them were pleasant. His primary suspicion was that they held weapons. There were weapons on board, of course. No one knew what to expect once they reached Aurora, but if there was some sort of animal life there, the weapons might be necessary, both for protection and for hunting. But Thomas suspected the containers held far worse weapons than rifles and handguns. If Havelar and his cronies were to establish their domain, they would need a sufficient armory, and back on Earth there was a range of weapons that would be able to perform such a role. So, although there might be other possibilities, weapons were what he thought most likely.

He knew the area where the containers were hidden well, because he'd been out there once before, just a few days ago. He had been nervous, knowing that one wrong step would result in the same fate that had befallen the poor technician. But he'd done what he intended to, and got safely back without anyone noticing. And now he had a tracker placed on each of the containers, which would allow him to know exactly where they landed, once they were safely down on Aurora. Even if Havelar managed to put them all safely down, there would be a slight chance that one of them could be stolen away. He didn't yet know how, but as always, he prepared to improvise. It had worked well so far.

Chapter 13

2244 ~ Outer 55 Cancri A system

Admiral Greg Hamilton stood on the bridge of the Exodus and looked out at the stars. 55 Cancri was far off in the distance, barely visible to the naked eye, and in just a few months, they would start waking the rest of the crew and passengers. At the moment, close to fifty people were awake, and although there was a mood of relief and joy as the journey seemed to draw to a close, most of those awake right now were just too busy to really savor these moments. For the last fifteen years, the magnetic sails had been deployed, and were giving the ship the necessary deceleration to be able to enter an orbit around Aurora. So far everything had gone according to plan, and Hamilton was relieved that no sudden malfunctions had occurred. After all, more than a century and a half had passed since they left Earth, so many things could have happened in that time. There had been the slingshots, which had put an enormous strain on the structure of the Exodus, the journey through the Oort Cloud, littered with comets and debris, a nerve-racking experience for those awake at the time, the encounter with a comet that cost the life of a brave technician, and other less costly incidents.

The next hurdle would be to find a stable orbit, and then of course the descent to the planet. They had gathered much more data on the planet itself during the course of the journey, although many questions still remained, such as what forms of life it contained. But there were more and more data coming in as to temperature and atmospheric conditions, and so far everything looked good, and the planet still looked habitable, although it was far too early to tell whether Aurora had a breathable atmosphere. There were so many other factors that were important about the atmosphere, and whether it was breathable was something that couldn't be fully determined until they were on the ground. Even if the composition was just right, they would have to determine whether it contained trace elements that could be harmful, or dangerous bacteria or spores, and a lot of other airborne elements that could only be detected up close.

Greg Hamilton had reason to be a happy man, but still he worried. Although there was still a lot to be done before they were safely in orbit, and even more before they were able to walk on their new home world, those challenges were not what worried him. The thing that concerned him was what kind of life they would create for themselves, once the bare necessities of survival were overcome. He knew that George Havelar had been appointed governor by the president, back in the twenty-first century, but he also knew that a lot of people questioned what kind of authority a president—long dead, on a world probably just as dead—had to give any sort of directions. He also knew that Havelar, although an assertive and powerful man, did have enemies. Not personally, as far as he knew, but as the representative of a system that had turned oppressive and inhuman in its last decades. And he felt torn. A military man to the core, Hamilton knew how important it was to have a chain of command when going into unknown territory. Who knew what dangers and obstacles they'd encounter? So having a set leadership from the start was important, and could prove the difference between a mission accomplished and an utter failure, which in this case could prove lethal, not just to the ones involved, but for an entire species. On the other hand, he'd never been comfortable with the way things had developed back on Earth, and although for the most part, he'd been a world apart from everything that had happened back home, he'd seen what had happened to civilian society. So perhaps it would have been better to start over from scratch, and have an elected leadership even before first landing. But the difficulty with that was that there were no good alternatives; no one to challenge Havelar and his Consortium allies. It was analogue to the situation in America when they left. In a one-party system, there could be no well-known, effective opposition, and that was also the case here. So in the end, they would have to go with the old system and its workings, until something else could grow to actually challenge the established system. He only hoped the transition would be smooth. What he feared the most was that Havelar and his crew would try to turn him and the rest of the military contingent into tools of oppression. Although he was old and experienced enough to withstand such a course, there would always be someone ready to take his place. And a military background, although very positive in the sense of commitment and ability to carry out dangerous and demanding tasks, always held a propensity for obedience and misunderstood loyalty. Under the proper conditions, that could easily turn them into willing tools of malice.

Waking up from Sleep the second time around was not nearly as bad as the last time. The first time she woke, about two decades into the journey through space, the experience had been more painful, and she had been coughing and spitting for almost half an hour, as her body tried to empty her lungs and stomach of fluids, a ripping, agonizing fight back to life from a near-death existence. Shivering cold, wet from the life-sustaining but nevertheless quite awful liquids that had surrounded her since leaving Earth. It had taken days before she felt normal again, and even then, the memory would occasionally make her shiver. Yes, she had quietly dreaded the moment she would have to experience all that again, back when she let herself slip into her second dreamless sleep, although the adventure, of course, had always taken precedence.

But for Maria Solis, the second waking couldn't have been farther from the horrors of the first time around. Her expectations were based on her knowledge at the time, and since then, something extraordinary, or maybe not so extraordinary, had happened; time had passed. A long time had passed. When she later thought back on it, she realized her surprise was due to a simple fact one should not overlook, namely the fact that human minds are shaped to expect the known. And the known at the time had been her own experience; anything else would have been theoretical. But by the time she was woken again, several lifetimes had passed, and the ongoing labor of the scientists and engineers and technicians, combined with the most advanced AI ever created, had developed a better way of reviving its sleeping inhabitants. For more than a century, that work had steadily progressed, and when considering the technological development in the last century back on Earth, there was no reason to expect any of it to be even remotely the same as it had been.

It could probably best be described as waking up, fully rested, on a sunny day in spring, to the smell of fresh-brewed coffee, in a house on the beach, where the sounds of seagulls would compete with the surf breaking on the smooth sands. Of course, it wasn't entirely like that, but that was how it felt anyway, and it was the best way to describe it, Maria thought. Nice. After a few minutes of coming to terms with where she was, and what she was doing there, she stood up from the soft bed, she couldn't describe it in any other way, and took the cotton-like blue coveralls laid out for her. She was alone in a square, warmly lit room, not spacious by any means, but unlike what she remembered from before Sleep, and there was a single door, through which she could hear subdued voices. She quickly got dressed and walked toward the door. For a second, she let her hand run across her shaven scalp. Why hadn't they found a way to fix that? She almost laughed out loud and shook her head at her girlish notions. It would grow back, of course, but she still felt naked without her hair. She paused before the door, then opened it and stepped out into the corridor.

Outside, she almost bumped into her parents. They seemed surprised, but happy to see her.

"Maria," her mother said, hugging her fiercely.

"We didn't think you'd be up yet. We've been out here for half an hour." Her father chuckled, while joining his wife and daughter in a loving group hug.

"It's probably easier on you young people. Me, I guess it took hours before I could even move. It was a whole lot easier than the first time, but my muscles were still sore and my joints stiff. Turns out your old man has gotten older after all." Maria smiled fondly at him. It seemed he had a point. His half-inch long hair showed a few more grey patches now. All of them had been awake once during the flight, which meant two years, and cryo sleep didn't completely halt metabolism, just slowed it considerably. From what she'd learned, they would all have aged from two to three years while deep in Sleep. That meant she would be what, thirty, thirty-one? Ramon's tablet pinged, and he looked down at it. At the same time, Isabella and Maria received messages on their tablets as well.

"Ah, it's a message on the common channel. There will be a big meeting tomorrow, for everyone to attend via the screens." There was nowhere to gather everyone on board, so such meetings would have to be conducted by everyone gathering in small groups in the various living quarters that each contained conference equipment.

"I guess there will be some info on what Aurora looks like," he said.

"So I guess that most people are already awake then?" Maria asked. Her father nodded, smiling, and Isabella took her hand.

"Actually, you were the last, Maria. Everyone's awake now."

"Let's all go to the viewing gallery," her father said.

"We can see Aurora from there. It's an amazing sight, Maria. Our new home." Somehow he looked like a schoolboy, his expression at least thirty years younger than his age. Maria couldn't help but laugh before she hugged her father again. Serious businessman or not, he had always been a lot of fun, she thought. The eight years of preparations, from when Devastator was discovered until the Exodus left Earth orbit, had taken a huge toll on him, but somehow he seemed to have regained his youthful energy as the burden of responsibility had been replaced by a spirit of adventure. She thought she'd never seen him as full of life and anticipation as now. She kissed him affectionately, while thinking how lucky she was. Most of the others on board had left someone back on Earth, and of course she had left friends as well, but she had her family around her, which was something few others had. And now she looked forward to her new life, and whatever discoveries awaited her on the new world.

Kenneth Taylor was standing in a crowded room, where the large screen on the wall showed an image of the main science lab. The man standing next to him was that young administrative employee of the Consortium, Thomas Dunn, whom he'd become acquainted with just before the Exodus left Earth orbit. A strange young man, Kenneth thought, but he sort of liked him. Even after talking to him several times, he still didn't know much about him though. It seemed Mr. Dunn was the kind of man who valued his privacy, and Kenneth respected that. It was a trait they both shared.

The camera zoomed in on a man about Kenneth's own age, obviously the admiral, who smiled beneath a thick mustache, and proceeded to introduce some of the other people standing beside him.

"Dr. Karin Svensson here, our astronomer, will explain what we have found so far when it comes to the star system and atmospheric conditions on Aurora. On her right, you have Professor Jeremiah Lowell, who will go through the findings on planetary conditions, geology, and so forth. My executive officer, Major Tina Hammer, will be leading the first landing party, and she will tell you a little of what will await you on the ground. Well, enough talking on my part, let me just tell you how pleased I am that we managed to get here." He took a brief pause.

"Aurora … It's been a hell of a journey … And it's not over yet. So let me just remind you to pay close attention to what is said here today. When we're entering the new world, there may be dangers that we've missed, but the more information you're able to absorb beforehand, the more prepared you will be for whatever may come." He smiled again and gestured toward the others.

"All right then, I think that's enough bullshit. Let's get down to business, shall we?" The first to take a step forward was Dr. Svensson, who gave the camera a brief nod as it zoomed in on her.

"As you should know by now, the 55 Cancri system consists of two separate stars; a yellow dwarf star and a smaller red dwarf star. If you've paid any attention to what was known at the time of our departure, you would know that the yellow dwarf, 55 Cancri A, is quite similar to the sun. It is smaller and slightly less massive than our sun, and so is cooler and less luminous. However, since Aurora is closer to its star than Earth was to our sun, the temperature on the ground will be about the same, possibly a just a little colder.

Now, the star has little or no variability and only low emission from its chromosphere. This is important, as it gives us a stable environment so to speak, with a very low chance of flares. We still know little about 55 Cancri B, as we have focused primarily on the star that will have the main impact on our destination planet. But what we know is that 55 Cancri B is a red dwarf star, located at an estimated mean distance of 1,065 AUs from its primary. One astronomical unit, for those who didn't pay attention, is equal to the mean distance between the sun and Earth. This star is both small and dark, compared to both the sun and the primary, but we will be able to see it at times, when its alignment and the atmospheric conditions on Aurora are just right." Kenneth hadn't seen the Swedish astronomer before, but he recognized her brisk and stern mannerism for what it was: insecurity and nervousness. She had stopped for a moment, and coughed lightly before she continued. Yes, she seemed nervous all right.

"Let's move on to the planetary system of 55 Cancri A then. So far, we have found seven planets, but we can't rule out the existence of more, even though they would likely be located at a very great distance from the star. Aurora is the fifth planet from the primary, and has a mean distance from the star of 0.92 AUs. It is a little smaller than Earth, with about 90 percent of Earth's gravity, which means you will feel lighter and stronger, at least initially, until your body adapts to the conditions. Its year has 325 days, and it rotates around its own axis in twenty-eight hours. That means we'll have longer days, while the years will be shorter. Aurora has an axial tilt that is somewhat less than that of Earth, but close enough that there will be seasonal variations.

"As to the other planets, the three closest to the star are gas giants, and too close to support life. The fourth, also a gas giant, lies within the habitable zone, and although it is covered in water clouds, it is not especially hospitable to humans, as it has no solid surface. It does have at least three moons though, and at least one of them has liquid water, and there might be life there. This is our closest neighborhood, so I guess we'll look into that once we're fully established on Aurora. Okay … The sixth planet is located at 5.74 AUs out, and has a mass of almost five times that of Jupiter. This is very good, because this planet's gravity will suck in a lot of the dangerous objects that would otherwise be drawn toward the star. Who knows what they might hit on their way." Kenneth thought of what had happened to Mars, and later to Earth itself. Yes, he thought, that sounds good.

"And at last, close to 10 AUs out, we have a rocky planet of about five Earth masses. This is an extremely cold, dead world, and we have not focused as much on it so far." She paused again, and looked at the admiral, who smiled and nodded for her to continue.

"So let's move on to atmospheric conditions. I guess you are all eager to know more about that. The science teams have just finished analyzing the data from the probes that were sent down when we first arrived. I'll go through the main results, and bear with me that we do not have all the data ready yet, but we do know a few things for certain at this point." She lifted her head from her notes, and looked straight into the camera for the first time, and then, surprisingly, a smile lit up her face.

"The atmosphere is not very different from Earth, and as we have always suspected, but didn't dare to believe until we came here, it is breathable." That brought cheers and applause from all the rooms where people were watching the presentation. Kenneth thought that breathing fresh air was something profoundly human, and the thought of wearing space suits for the rest of their lives had always been a little depressing, at least subconsciously.

"All right, all right, this is great news, I agree. Just … Let's not get all carried away yet." The noise subsided as the Swedish astronomer carried on.

"So far, the probes have found no dangerous microorganisms or trace elements that would constitute a hazard to humans, but nevertheless, we have to be careful. So what will happen is this. The first landing party will be wearing airtight suits, just in case we have overlooked something. We are taking no chances here; there is too much at stake. So Hammer and her team will take a lot of samples that will need to be analyzed before we can be certain of anything. You should expect to be wearing facemasks for some time. These masks will filter out any organic material, which is what we fear the most. It seems the air itself won't harm us.

"And lastly, I want to mention that back in 2078, while most of you were in Selection, we found that there is photosynthesis at work here. That led us to believe that there is vegetation, and this has now been confirmed. There are other signs of life too, such as heat signatures recorded by the probes, but that is as much as we can possibly detect at the moment. There seem to be no structures that are in any way built or created, so the likelihood of intelligent life is low. But again, I will not rule it out, as it may just be different from what we associate with intelligence." She took a step back and the camera shifted to Professor Lowell.

"Right, first of all, I'd like to say to y'all that geology is a crucial element as to the long-term viability of inhabiting this planet. What we wished for when we came here was an active world. Earth is active, which means that the core is alive, which is an important element in giving the planet its magnetic field, a feature that has many uses, but most importantly, protects Earth from solar flares, which would otherwise cause radiation that could kill all life on the planet. We have found this on Aurora as well, which is a good thing. It means that when 55 Cancri A flares, which isn't as frequently as the sun, but still, we have something like a force field that will protect us. And we have plate tectonics. There seem to be both active volcanoes and tectonic activity down there. Less than Earth, but enough to enrich the surface with resources and nutrients that support life.

"There are four major continents, which seem to have some major differences. We'll need to decide on where to land, as that will be our home for a long time, until we are able to explore more of the planet." He brought up a roughly sketched map, and held it up for the camera.

"As you can see, there is a large amount of water here. In fact, about half the planet is covered by water. The rest is mainly split up between the four continents, although there are other landmasses as well, a couple of mini continents and several large islands. Now, the eastern continent, which we've decided to call Cerula, consists mainly of rocky deserts, highlands, and mountains, with one large inland sea. It doesn't seem to have as much vegetation as the others, but there are numerous indications that there may be large deposits of important resources in the ground. The northwestern continent, named Rossi, has an area in the south with dense forests and rivers, while the greater part is covered in ice. Just south of this continent is a smaller landmass, Verdi. We chose to call it a continent because it appears to have a different topography altogether, that seems more temperate, with varied topography. Here we found grasslands, rivers, mountains, forests ... The last continent, Viola, is the smallest, and it is separated from the others by the planet's largest ocean. It is located west of Verdi, on the same latitude, and seems to have a similar topography."

The camera shifted again. This time it was the executive officer, Major Tina Hammer, who greeted the camera. She went on to tell them how they were planning to enter the atmosphere of Aurora and make the first landing, and the importance of choosing a good spot that could support the population, as they all would gradually be transported down to the surface. By then, Kenneth was lost in thought, and when Tina finally finished, he discovered that he couldn't remember anything she had said.

Chapter 14

2245 ~ Aurora orbit

There were four shuttles on board, and they were outfitted with chemical rockets, very similar to those that had been used for carrying people and materials up into Earth orbit. The design was nothing groundbreaking; it was simple, sturdy, and built to last. The shuttles were capable of carrying thirty adults, including the pilots, and had an automatic glider system that adapted its flight to the characteristics of the atmosphere and gravity of Aurora, and by itself, it was capable of identifying—and avoiding— risky terrain, such as oceans, rocky areas, and mountains, taking them safely to ground. The automatic system ensured a safe landing and freed the shuttle pilot for other tasks, such as scouting for terrain that would be suitable for long-term habitability, which was a different challenge altogether. The pilot could take manual control at any given time, and she could also alter the designated landing spots the automatic system proposed. This was crucial on this first flight, as the spot they chose would likely be where they would set up their initial camp, which would soon grow into a colony. They didn't have enough fuel to search all over the planet to find the perfect spot, so when they found something that looked good enough, for both landing and long-term habitability, that would be where they would land.

As Tina buckled up, she glanced over at her copilot, Lieutenant Henry Carroll. She had chosen him personally, knowing that he was capable and steady, and quick to react in an emergency. He was also her friend. Now he was doing the final checks and everything looked fine. As the hatch was closed, he smiled at her and nodded affirmatively. They were ready. In a minute, the shuttle would be released from the Exodus, and the attitude thrusters would separate them from the mother ship. They silently counted down the seconds.

"All right, folks. Hang on. Three, two, one." There was a rattling sound, and a bang followed by another and another and another. That was the attitude thrusters, separating the shuttle from the mother ship. Tina felt a pull as the shuttle glided out, away from the Exodus and into its own orbit.

"That's it. We're clear. Initiating auto pilot." She toggled a switch and the attitude thrusters kept working to adjust the shuttle to its projected course.

The new world came closer into view as the shuttle gained speed. They were flying over the night side of the planet now, and it was utterly black. So different from Earth, where the night would be lit up all over the planet. The marks of human civilization. Tina enjoyed the sensation, but kept a close watch on the displays. It was an old habit of hers, never trusting the automatic system completely.

There were six passengers, scientists all. They would assess the landing site, from potential for agriculture to meteorological conditions to running tests on the local vegetation, sampling the air, and a whole set of other tasks. She didn't know each of the scientists personally, but she trusted they were the best at what they did.

"Okay, ready for retro burn. Three, two, one." There was a kick in the back, and they were pressed into their couches. They could feel the shuttle changing directions. The retro system was designed to shed their velocity, in order to take it out of orbit and let it fall toward the atmosphere of Aurora. After more than a century, it still functioned, just as the technicians who'd inspected it said it would. The retro burn ended abruptly, and they were thrown forward into their straps.

"All good, Major," Henry said. They were no longer in orbit. Now the shuttle was falling toward the planet, small bursts from the attitude thrusters adjusting its alignment and course so that the nose pointed in the direction of descent. A few minutes later, the shuttle tipped up, so that it flew belly first, where the large heat shield would protect them when they entered the atmosphere.

Then they felt it. Gravity. They were entering the atmosphere. At the same time, they saw the first light of day, as dawn quickly came closer. The view was suddenly obscured, as the colors of the burning plasma filled the air around the shuttle. Tina and Henry looked at each other, and Tina could see the concern on her copilot's face. They both knew this was a critical phase. The shuttles were designed from years of experience with Earth's atmospheric entry, but no one really knew how that would work here. In theory, it should be fine, with everything adjusted to the conditions of Aurora's atmosphere, but you never knew. As the shuttle shook more violently, Tina felt sweat trickle down her back. There were no guarantees, no certainty, and this was something quite different from flying scramjets across North Africa.

Then, just like that, the plasma dissipated to reveal blue sky with scattered clouds around them. Somewhere, while covered in the burning plasma, they had crossed the terminator into daytime. The shuttle shook a little as it adjusted to its new surroundings. They were flying. No longer falling, but actually flying. They were still high up, so the horizon still showed a curve, but they were able to see contours of the landscape beneath them. They were flying toward Verdi, where they assumed they would be able to find a spot where both landing requirements and possibility of long-term habitation would match. Things were moving very quickly now. They flew across a mountainous landscape that had to be somewhere in the western regions of Cerula. As their descent continued, they passed the coastline and beneath them were the vast expanses of ocean. Tina recognized the features from the map that Professor Lowell had shown them. It shouldn't be long now.

After a few minutes, they could see land in the distance. The shoreline approached quickly, and once they lowered the landing gear, the shuttle started shaking again.

"That's it," Henry said. Tina could see it now too; the grasslands were right in front of them. The landing site was an expanse of grasslands with a forest to the south, and a river running just north of it, while north of the grasslands there was a region of low mountains. The coast would be to the east of their landing site.

They were flying low now, just a hundred meters, eighty, seventy …

"This is it," Tina said into the comms, so that everyone could hear. "We're going in for landing." She gently pushed at a handle, and the landing gear touched ground. Carefully she let the weight of the shuttle come down. The shuttle skipped a few times before finally settling down, speeding across the landscape. Then there was a loud bang as the chutes deployed. The shuttle slowed, and as it came to a halt, Tina realized she had been holding her breath, and she let it out. Henry had a wide grin on his face as he released his secondary handle, and looked at the readings on the displays. All good, it seemed. The shuttle would be operational again in just sixteen hours, the time it took to reload the batteries and refill the rockets, an automated process that converted atmospheric components into rocket fuel. Tina peeked out as she reported back into the comms.

"Exodus, this is shuttle. We are safely down."

Setting up camp was hard labor, and Thomas Dunn breathed heavily under the weight of a crate filled with some kind of lab equipment. The first landing had been a success yesterday, and now they had the first results from the soil and air samples taken. They were told that they would be able to plant edible crops here from the seeds brought from Earth, as soon as they had the camp ready and everybody settled in. That would be even harder work, as most of it would have to be done before winter set in. The scientists had given them some idea of what Aurora winter would be like, and although it would be comparable to certain parts of Earth, it wouldn't be comfortable. Thomas wasn't sure how to interpret that, but one thing was for sure; you didn't want to be caught out in the open on a cold winter night in these parts. But it was still late spring, and the air felt nice and warm against his exposed neck. He resisted the temptation to remove his facemask. He knew he would be able to breathe the air, and it would have felt so good, but the scientists had told them all to make sure they kept them on at all times until they had the air-tight shelters ready, so he did. He wasn't much for respecting authorities, but this mandate he would stick with. Who knew what kind of bugs he would catch if he didn't.

He caught a glimpse of the shrink, Taylor, and chuckled to himself, as the older man was obviously having a harder time of it than he. Sweating hard, while carrying a piece of one of the containers that would be used as living quarters, Taylor had to stop to catch his breath every ten steps. They had been told the lower gravity would make them all feel super fit, at least initially, but at the moment, he didn't think Taylor would agree. As Dunn carried a crate over to the biology team, who of course had to be at the other end of the campsite, he thought about the shrink. An interesting fellow actually; so careful with his words, Thomas thought. He didn't know where the man stood, but obviously he wasn't one of Havelar's cronies; he would have known if he was in the inner circle, but of course that didn't mean he was to be trusted. The plan had been designed so that no one knew who had been picked by the senator and his people, and who were thought of as loyal to the Andrews regime. Even so, Taylor didn't seem to fit the bill in either direction. And considering it, perhaps he didn't belong to either camp. Perhaps the psychologist would turn out to be something else entirely.

The campsite was located in the far east of the continent they had named Verdi, on a large expanse of grasslands, not far from the coastline. Just to the north there was a wide river, and Thomas thought that once the immediate tasks on site were covered, they should try to see if Aurora had any fishing opportunities. From what he knew of fishing back on Earth, it looked promising. Of course, no one knew whether fish or anything that resembled fish even existed on Aurora, although the biologists believed the waters surely held some kind of life. But he would certainly go check it out as soon as possible.

North of the river, there were mountains that would probably protect them somewhat from the northern winds the meteorologists had said they should expect come winter. The geologists suspected the area to be rich in minerals as well, and the sooner they could get started on mining their own resources the better. He could see the peaks from here, still covered in snow. He wondered whether they had glaciers or some kind of snow up there throughout summer too. The lower temperature and the altitude made it entirely possible, even though the highest couldn't be more than around two thousand meters.

When Thomas looked to the south, the only thing he could see was more grassland. But he knew that there were large forests in that direction, from what they had told him. The rough maps they all had on their tablets now showed the forests to be about a three or four-day walk away. To the west, there would be grasslands and sparse forest in between lakes and a few hills or mountains. It seemed the terrain varied more to the west, and beyond the first lakes no one really knew much of what to expect just yet.

The site itself stretched over an area of more than two square kilometers. They would have several housing areas, where all living quarters would have at least one air-tight room, and there would be communal air-filtering facilities that would provide these rooms with clean filtered air. In the southern end of the site would be a runway for the shuttles that would remain valuable means of transportation, both around the area, as well as to and from the Exodus, which would remain in orbit, to serve as a communications / weather / scientific satellite. From time to time, someone might need to get up there for maintenance or some scientific work that couldn't be conducted on the ground, and the Exodus had great equipment for astronomy, which would be used for getting to know the planetary neighborhood.

Getting the fusion reactors that would provide electricity for the colonists up and running was one of the highest priorities. At the moment, the first one was actually being assembled, just north of the site, close to where the greenhouses would be situated. South of the reactors there would be a large administrative building and a hospital. The hospital would be the only building, at least for the time being, that would be completely air tight, with filtered air in the entire building. And of course, the labs of the scientists would be clustered together, somewhat resembling a university campus. That was where Thomas was standing right now, in the western part of the site, too far from the shuttle field, he thought. After unloading the crate, he walked over to the nearest person for a quick breather.

"So, how's it going over here? You found anything interesting yet?" he said as he leaned against a stack of crates still unopened. A girl, or rather a woman, probably somewhere around thirty, eyed him sideways. She seemed to have something else on her mind, but as she was the only one there, it was obvious the question had been directed at her. She didn't say anything for a couple of seconds, and Thomas noticed that she had beautiful eyes, and the rest didn't look too bad either, with close-cropped black hair and Latino features. Judging from her hair—or lack thereof, she must have been one of the last ones to wake up, he thought. Of course, the facemask hid most of her face.

"Well, that's not really my area of expertise, but … I'm working on agriculture, and that seems promising … Ah, there seems to be a bit of wildlife here actually. The first thing they found was some kind of insect, well, several kinds actually, that live right here on the ground. Kind of similar to beetles, just really small, so I guess most people haven't noticed them yet. And then there are the mosquitoes and bees, or whatever we decide to call them. There seem to be a lot of them further inland. There is actually a team of four biologists exploring the area just west of here as we speak." He reached out a hand toward her.

"I'm Thomas. Dunn. Administration." She took his hand, and shook it lightly.

"Maria Solis," she said. Solis. That would make her Ramon's daughter, Thomas thought. Ramon Solis was one of the head figures of the Consortium, but even so, he didn't seem close to Havelar. Deeply Consortium entwined of course, but a different person altogether.

"So, any other life forms around?" he continued. "Any proper aliens?" he winked at her, and he could see her smile under the mask.

"You know, Mr. Dunn ... we are the aliens here." Hmm, he thought. She's teasing.

"Come on now, you know what I mean," Thomas pushed on, half joking.

"All right then. Well, to answer your question, no. Not intelligent life, or at least not as we believe intelligent life would behave. We did find several tracks of some kind of large species right next to the shuttle field, and there have been infrared sightings of living things both to the north and south. From the size of mice to horses. But no sightings yet though. And there are large CO_2 emissions from the plains out west that cannot be anything other than living beings. But it's early still. Most of us came today. We haven't even got all the equipment down from the Exodus yet. I guess there will be new findings every day, as we explore the area more." He nodded, and decided he would talk some more with her later. He took out his mittens; it was chilly, even this time of year, so he put them on.

"Well, I'll get back to my crates now. Got a lot of stuff to move before we're done for the day. See you later." Then he turned away, and walked toward the shuttle field.

Walking back, he thought of the secret containers still secured to the Exodus. He had placed trackers on all of them, and knew they hadn't been moved yet. Whatever they contained, he would make sure that when the time came, he would be ready to go out on a little field trip of his own. The containers were too large to be placed in the shuttles, so they had to be moved from the Exodus to Aurora in some other fashion. Perhaps they were able to land by themselves? Anyway, if they held weapons, as he suspected, getting a hold of them could prove the difference between tyranny and freedom, and even though he doubted that he could secure them all, somehow he would make damn sure that Havelar didn't get all of them. Maybe he could even steal one or more away. That would take accomplices of course, and he still didn't know whom to trust. It would be a gamble, whatever he did, but he suspected the time for caution would come to an end, sooner or later. But not today. Thomas Dunn would be patient.

Epilogue

2245 ~ Aurora

It was their first night on Aurora, and everybody was gathered at the shuttle field, close to the safety of their three shuttles. When it came time to sleep, they would spend the night inside, with guards posted on the outside, and two infrared scanners continuously searching for anything that might constitute a threat. With the latest radar and motion-sensor technology, they should be safe enough. They hadn't discovered anything dangerous so far, but better to err on the safe side.

Maria Solis still hadn't gotten used to eating with the facemask on; it still felt awkward. You had to hold your breath as you opened some sort of lid where you could push the food in by little pieces. Then you had to wait for two seconds, as the sterilization system made sure the food was completely decontaminated, before another lid opened on the inside, and the food could be pushed into your mouth. It felt sterile and cumbersome, but for now they just had to get used to it. She quietly giggled to herself, thinking how gross eating anything with gravy or sauce would be. Drinking was easier, since they just inserted a straw, and as long as it wasn't too hot, that worked for soup as well. She imagined there would be a lot of soup.

She had a good feeling, although there were concerns on her mind as well. But mostly it felt good. They were the first humans to spend the night on Aurora. Thinking about the thrill of exploration made her think of her grandfather. He would have been so excited to have had such an opportunity.

The first landing party led by Major Hammer had returned to the Exodus, once the samples were all taken, and the shuttle rockets were recharged. They had all returned on the second flight down, with more passengers and equipment, as they were eager to continue their work. Hamilton had allowed it, and put Hammer in charge, as civilian authority wouldn't take over until all passengers were on the ground. Two more shuttles had returned with them, carrying as many as they could carry, including Maria and her father. One shuttle remained back on the Exodus, as a safety precaution in case something happened on the ground. After all, most of the people were still on the mother ship, and it would be weeks before everybody was down on Aurora. By that time, all the living quarters would be up, with the air filtering system and the first reactor online. It would be hard work, but by early summer, they should have crops planted and most of the science and exploration projects up and running.

Suddenly Maria heard a noise from far away. It was a deep rumble, resembling a lion's roar, although deeper. Though they hadn't seen much yet, it being the first day and all, from everything they had discovered so far, the planet seemed to be teeming with life. She looked forward to exploring her new home, and wondered what their life on Aurora would be like. She turned and looked at her father, sitting right next to her, a little back from the campfire. Obviously, he hadn't heard anything. He looked distant now, and she smiled inside her mask. Her mother was back on the Exodus, and she probably had that very same expression right now. They didn't cope well with being apart. She knew she was privileged, being here in the first place. Even more so, as most people didn't have their family around them. That was due to her parents being so high up in the Consortium hierarchy, of course, and knowing that had a bitter aftertaste. But who was she to complain? She did, however, suspect there would be a price to pay, since all that money that helped fund the Exodus project back on Earth would be worth nothing now that they had reached their final destination. Havelar would expect nothing short of obedience and strict loyalty from every Consortium associate and their families once he took charge. And how could her parents object to that, really? After all, the Consortium had taken her family away from the disaster that had awaited them on Earth, and given them a new chance.

"What is it, dear?" she heard her father say as she stared into the flames. It was her time to be far away now, lost deep in her own thoughts. She smiled again, and regarded him fondly.

"Nothing, Dad. Just wondering what happened to everybody back on Earth. I miss Elle … Aunt Lorena and Uncle Esteban …" She took a deep breath and her father gave her a knowing look. They both knew the odds. Of course, a century and a half later none of them would be alive, even if they had survived Devastator's impact. So, for better or worse, all they had now was each other, which was more than most had.

"Dad," she finally said. "Why did they call it Aurora? No one ever told us at Selection, and we were all so busy anyways." Her father's face lit up, and she saw that familiar twinkle in his eyes that she'd learned to recognize even as a kid.

"Aurora …" her father began. "Aurora was the Roman goddess of dawn. A new day … Hope, new beginnings … I don't know if that's why they chose that name, but I like to think so." Maria nodded and thought of what this had all been about. What was it, if not hope? A new beginning?

"I like that," she said.

She was deep in thought again when she noticed Havelar and a few of his people waving at her father. He saw it too, and rose with a sigh.

"I just hope we can do better this time," he said quietly, before he walked over to the head of the Consortium, soon to be governor of Aurora. Looking at her father, Maria thought he looked more subdued. Still, what he had said made her feel a deep sense of hope.

"This time, we make our own world," she whispered to herself, watching the flames of the campfire light up the night. The first night of their new life on Aurora.

Watch out for part 2 of the Exodus Trilogy

AURORA

www.christensenwriting.com

About the author

Andreas Christensen is a Norwegian writer who writes primarily science fiction and fantasy.

He has a degree in Psychology from the Norwegian University of Science and Technology, and his professional background is mainly from public service.

When he's not writing he's probably spending time with Siri and Jonas, or working (writing is not work, it's a whole bag of fun, sitting in front of the computer and making stuff up!)

Andreas has a weakness for cats, coffee and up untill recently, books so heavy he'd need a separate suitcase in order to carry them every time he travelled. Luckily, the world has changed, and the suitcase has now been replaced by an e-reader.

More from Andreas Christensen:

christensenwriting.com

amazon.com/author/andreaschristensen

twitter.com/achr75

facebook.com/christensenwriting

Bibliography

Exodus

The first installment of the Exodus Trilogy, a space opera of hope in the face of the greatest disaster in history.

The Tunnel

A short story about a man who finds himself in a situation in which the entire world around him has changed.

The Tribe

A short story set in the world of The Tunnel. In a world where only the strong survive, the ruthless may find opportunity to take advantage of the weak. And fighting predators can be extremely risky...

Valerian's Company

A fantasy of dark deeds and ruthless justice.

Made in the USA
Monee, IL
11 November 2020